THE WHITE MOUNTAIN

ALSO BY ROBERT GOLDSBOROUGH

NERO WOLFE MYSTERIES
Murder in E Minor
Death on Deadline
Fade to Black
The Bloodied Ivy
The Last Coincidence
Silver Spire
The Missing Chapter
Archie Meets Nero Wolfe—A Prequel
Murder in the Ball Park
Archie in the Crosshairs
Stop the Presses!
Murder Stage Left
The Battered Badge
Death of an Art Collector
Archie Goes Home
Trouble at the Brownstone
The Missing Heiress

SNAP MALEK CHICAGO MYSTERIES
Three Strikes You're Dead
Shadow of the Bomb
A Death in Pilsen
A President in Peril
Terror at the Fair
Stairway to Nowhere & Other Stories

THE WHITE MOUNTAIN

A Nero Wolfe Mystery

Robert Goldsborough

MYSTERIOUSPRESS.COM

OPEN ROAD

INTEGRATED MEDIA
NEW YORK

ISBN: 979-8-3372-0190-0

Published in 2025 by MysteriousPress.com/Open Road Integrated Media, Inc.
180 Maiden Lane
New York, NY 10038
www.openroadmedia.com

To Janet, for her unfailing support

over more than six decades

To the Reader . . .

This story is in essence an homage to Nero Wolfe's creator, Rex Stout. Mr. Stout's novel *The Black Mountain*, had Wolfe and Archie Goodwin traveling to Montenegro in the Balkans to hunt down the killer of Wolfe's oldest friend, Marko Vukcic.

I felt our protagonists should have another opportunity to travel beyond the borders of the United States, and because this tale centers on Wolfe's superb and troubled chef, Swiss-born Fritz Brenner, Switzerland in general and Geneva in particular seemed like an ideal setting for the narrative.

THE WHITE MOUNTAIN

CHAPTER 1

It was a normal weekday morning in Nero Wolfe's old brown-stone on Manhattan's West Thirty-Fifth Street during this, the twelfth year after the end of World War II. I sat at the small table in the kitchen reading the *New York Times* while Fritz Brenner, chef extraordinaire, served me hot buttermilk wheat cakes off the griddle, one at a time.

Those wheat cakes, along with black coffee, squeezed orange juice, a bowl of raspberries in cream, and scrambled eggs, constituted my typical breakfast, while Wolfe, as was his wont, consumed an essentially similar meal upstairs in his bedroom. Outwardly, it seemed that all was right with the world, but with this exception:

The Swiss-born Fritz, normally the most genial of men, had not been genial for the last few days. At first, I attributed his dark mood to a possible argument with Wolfe over whether to use onions in shad roe in casserole—Fritz was for it, Wolfe against. But that kind of a minor flare-up usually lasted no more than a day, not likely to cause the kind of despondency that engulfed Fritz.

I asked him more than once if something was troubling him and got only a shrug and a look that suggested he preferred not to respond. I hadn't brought the subject up to Wolfe but, before the morning was over, we were to learn what was bedeviling the man whose place in the brownstone was one of the household's most stabilizing presences.

After breakfast, I was in the office with a last cup of coffee and sorting through the morning mail, then stacking it on Wolfe's desk blotter for his perusal. After the nine-to-eleven session with his precious ten thousand orchids up in the plant room on the roof, he strode into the office, asking as he invariably did if I had slept well, and pushed the buzzer on his desk to ring for beer. I answered in the affirmative as Fritz entered with a stein and two chilled bottles of Remmers beer.

Wolfe nodded his thanks, usually the signal for Fritz to return to the kitchen, but he remained and turned toward Wolfe, clearing his throat.

"Yes, Fritz?"

"I need to talk to you, sir," he said, a slight quaver in his voice.

"With or without Mr. Goodwin present?"

"Oh, Archie can stay, of course," he said, coloring slightly.

"Very well," Wolfe said. "Sit down, Fritz."

"Well, I . . ." Fritz saw himself as hired help and, in my memory, he had never sat in the office.

"Sit down," Wolfe repeated firmly, dipping his chin in the direction of one of the yellow chairs in front of his desk.

Fritz perched on the front few inches of the seat, swallowing hard.

"What do you need to talk about?" Wolfe asked in a non-threatening tone. "You have our attention."

"I have a cousin in Switzerland, in Geneva, Paul. He is my closest relative still alive."

"You have mentioned him on occasion. I believe he captains a vessel on Lac Leman," Wolfe said, turning to me. "Archie, Americans call that body of water Lake Geneva."

"Yes, Mr. Wolfe," Fritz said. "He has had that job for many years."

"And now. . . ?"

Fritz was trying with mixed success to compose himself. "And now, I've had no word from him, nothing for three weeks."

"Are the two of you in the habit of communicating frequently?"

"We write letters, of course, usually weekly. I have written him three letters now with no response. When I hadn't heard from him for so long, I made a long-distance call to his telephone number, not from this house but from outside, and was told it was not in operation. I feel I must go to Geneva."

Although he didn't show it, that statement jarred Wolfe. Fritz is as important to him as his orchids or his books or maybe even me. And the thought of his not being in the kitchen and preparing meals that would be the envy of the most discriminating of palates was unthinkable.

"May I make a suggestion, Fritz?"

"Yes, sir."

"I know a man in London who is a private investigator. His name is Geoffrey Hitchcock. I value his abilities, and he has been of help in the past when Archie and I were in need of information from the other side of the Atlantic. I am prepared to ask that he travel to Geneva as quickly as he is able and to seek your cousin. Would that be agreeable to you?"

Wolfe had put Fritz in something of a bind. He clearly wanted to go to Switzerland, but he found it hard to say no to Wolfe's offer. He nodded and said, "Yes, sir, thank you. I will go back to the kitchen now."

"Before you go, I believe your cousin's surname is Bernard. Am I correct?"

"Yes, he is Paul Bernard, my late uncle's son. He is divorced and has no children, so he lives alone in a Geneva apartment."

"Do you have Mr. Bernard's current address and do you have the name of the company that employs him?"

"Yes, I will write them both down for you," he said as I handed him a pencil and a sheet of paper.

After Fritz left, I swiveled to face Wolfe. "Do you think Hitchcock is up to the job?" I asked.

"I happen to know that he is fluent in French, Archie, and as you are aware, he can be tenacious and thorough, as he has shown in the past."

"Okay, I guess it's worth a try. I know you want to keep Fritz on the job."

"Speaking of which, I need to see how he is coming with the mushroom and almond omelet that is to be our lunch." With that, Wolfe rose and turned in the direction of the kitchen to play his role as the overseer of the brownstone's culinary arts.

CHAPTER 2

After lunch, Wolfe and I were back in the office with coffee. "Archie, what time is it in London?" he asked.

That is my boss for you. He is a certifiable genius, but his gaps in knowledge in areas like local geography and global time zones show his lack of concern for what he considers too mundane to trouble him.

"They are five hours ahead of us this time of year, so it's"—I checked my watch—"about eight thirty there."

"Just so. Please telephone Mr. Hitchcock."

Anticipating the order, I already had pulled the London number from my file and placed the call through a long-distance operator, motioning Wolfe to pick up his instrument. After hearing several female voices and some static, I heard, "Hitchcock here."

"Good evening, Mr. Hitchcock. This is Nero Wolfe."

"Ah, Mr. Wolfe, so good to hear your voice. I trust you are well, sir."

"I am, thank you. Are you occupied with business?"

"Not as much as I would like of late. But the tides, they do ebb and flow, as I'm sure you know."

"I do indeed. Would you be interested in a commission?"

"I just might be."

"It would entail a trip to Geneva."

"A lovely lakeside city indeed and one I am somewhat familiar with. I have been there several times, for both business and pleasure."

"I suspected as much," Wolfe replied, proceeding to fill Hitchcock in on all that we knew about Paul Bernard.

"I can leave for Geneva tomorrow morning, Mr. Wolfe," Hitchcock said. "I assume you expect daily reports."

"Your assumption is correct," Wolfe replied. "If I am unavailable when you telephone, Mr. Goodwin will be reachable. He is on the line with me now."

"Mr. Goodwin! I shall be happy to keep you and Mr. Wolfe apprised of all developments."

I thanked him and, before signing off, Wolfe assured our agent that all expenses, including telephone and cable charges, would be covered.

"Now we wait," I told Wolfe.

And wait we did. For two days we heard nothing from Hitchcock and on the third morning, when I was in the office typing letters that Wolfe had dictated the day before, I got a transatlantic call.

"Good morning, Mr. Goodwin, this is Geoffrey Hitchcock."

"I recognize your voice. And the connection is very clear."

"Yes, improvements continue to be made in technology. I am afraid I have little to report to you and Mr. Wolfe, which is why I have not telephoned sooner."

"I am sorry to hear that."

"I went to Mr. Bernard's address and learned from the concierge that she had not seen him for at least two weeks, possibly longer. She had no idea where he might have gone and she said he had not been behaving strangely.

"Then I went to the steamship line where he is a captain and the supervisor I talked to essentially said the same thing as the concierge. Mr. Bernard had been an exemplary employee over his long years of service, but one day several weeks ago he did not show up for his shift and has not been heard from since. And according to the supervisor, none of his colleagues seem to know anything about his possible whereabouts."

Hitchcock went on to tell me he visited one of the local newspapers and was told by reporters that there have been no recent reports of missing persons and no bodies have been found in the lake over the last several months. He also visited a couple of bars where ship crew members hang out and none of them said they knew what had happened to Bernard.

I told Hitchcock to leave a number where he can be reached and said I would ask Wolfe if he had further instructions.

"I certainly won't charge Mr. Wolfe for the drinks I had in those lakeside pubs," he told me. "He should not have to finance my alcoholic endeavors."

"I don't agree," I responded. "That was an essential part of your intelligence gathering, even though you had very little success. I will report to Mr. Wolfe."

When Wolfe came down at eleven after his morning session with the orchids, I filled him in on Hitchcock's report. After ringing for beer, he scowled and nodded to Fritz, who had come in as usual with two chilled bottles and a stein. After he had gone back to the kitchen, Wolfe sighed deeply.

"Very well, I see no alternative than to send Mr. Hitchcock back to London and to tell Fritz he is free to go to Geneva. Do you concur?"

"I do. Even if he has no more success than Hitchcock did, he needs to satisfy himself. Or maybe, just maybe, his knowledge of Geneva and the general area will lead him to uncover the mystery of the missing cousin. What will you do to replace him in the kitchen?"

Another sigh. "This will be a challenge we must face. Please get Felix on the telephone."

Wolfe was referring to Felix Martin of Rusterman's Restaurant. A bit of background here: Rusterman's, arguably the finest dining spot in Manhattan, had for years been owned and operated by Marko Vukcic, the closest friend Nero Wolfe ever had, dating to their boyhood in Montenegro. When Marko was murdered, Wolfe and I went to Montenegro in search of his killer.* After Wolfe was made the executor of Marko's estate, which of course included Rusterman's, he selected Felix to oversee the operations, which the man has continued to do with Wolfe's oversight and his periodic visits to the restaurant.

I dialed the number from memory and Felix answered on the second ring while Wolfe picked up his receiver. "Felix, I have a favor to ask."

"Yes, Mr. Wolfe." Felix has always been in awe of Wolfe, eager to please to the point of being obsequious.

"Fritz must leave us on family business for an undetermined amount of time and I am in need of a replacement to serve in his stead at my home."

After a prolonged silence, Felix spoke. "I am not sure I can suggest someone who would be satisfactory."

---

* *The Black Mountain* by Rex Stout, 1954

"What about Leon Farber? I have heard you speak highly of his work."

"Yes, we could . . . we could part with him for some period. Do you know how long you would need him?"

"I do not, but I am hoping that for however long we may require his services, it will not be an undue imposition upon you."

"We will get along, Mr. Wolfe. As you are well aware, we have a fine staff."

"Thank you, Felix. I will inform you when I know more about Fritz's absence."

"So, do you see bringing this guy in as a great sacrifice?" I asked Wolfe when we had hung up.

"This is not what I would have wished, but do you agree that we owe it to Fritz to support this trip?"

"I do and in spades. I don't have to tell you he hasn't been himself at all lately and, with the report we got from Hitchcock, his anxiety will only increase. Although he hasn't spent much time there in recent years, he at least knows a lot about Geneva and its environs and may be able to be more effective than Hitchcock was in figuring out what's going on."

"We are in agreement," Wolfe said. "Please ask Fritz to come in, and I will share Hitchcock's report with him."

Overall, Fritz took the news pretty well, nodding a couple of times and otherwise remaining stoic. "I have arranged for a replacement in your absence," Wolfe told him, "and I will of course cover your expenses to Switzerland."

"No, sir!" Fritz said, springing to his feet. "I have money, and I will pay my way."

Wolfe dipped his chin a quarter of an inch. "Very well. I will see if Leon Farber from Rusterman's can start in the kitchen tomorrow morning. Would you be willing to meet with him and help him to get started?"

"I would, Mr. Wolfe."

"Good. Perhaps you can secure a flight to Switzerland sometime tomorrow afternoon or evening. Mr. Goodwin can help you make arrangements and he can drive you to the airport as well."

"I will talk to you later," I told Fritz. "We can begin to make the arrangements this afternoon."

"Thank you very much, Archie," he said in a somber tone, standing and leaving the office. There was a lunch to finish preparing.

<h1 style="text-align:center">CHAPTER 3</h1>

After Wolfe and I finished our meal, I got on the horn to Larry Marks, a travel agent Lily Rowan and I have used several times to help plan our jaunts to Norway, the Caribbean, and Paris, among other destinations.

"Good to hear your voice, Archie," he said. "Just where are you and the lovely Miss R. going this time? Tahiti, perhaps? Maybe the Austrian Alps? Or even sailing on the Nile?"

"If only that were the case, Larry. No, this time I'm looking to get a flight to Geneva, and as quickly as possible."

"For you?"

"No, for Fritz Brenner, who is the—"

"I know who Fritz is, Archie. You've raved to me about his great meals before. Let me see what I can do," he said, and I heard pages turning. "Just how soon are we talking about?"

"Is sometime late tomorrow realistic?"

"Hmm. Yes . . . I think so. Ah, here's one what leaves Idlewild at five p.m. for London. There he will has to change planes for Switzerland, getting to Geneva at noon the next day. There are no New York-to-Geneva direct flights."

"No, I suppose that's asking too much. All right, book it. Can Fritz pay at the airport."

"He can indeed. He's last name is Brenner, right?"

"Bingo."

"Consider it done."

That taken care of, I phoned Felix at Rusterman's and arranged to pick up Leon Farber at the restaurant and bring him to the brownstone to meet with Wolfe and Fritz. I had only seen Farber at a distance in Rusterman's and had never spoken to him. When we drove away from the restaurant, I tried to make conversation, but he seemed unwilling to say much.

He didn't present an impressive figure—short, balding, stoop-shouldered, and tight-lipped. I had to wonder how he and Wolfe would get along.

I parked in front of the brownstone and walked Farber up the stairs to the door, which Fritz swung open before I could ring. The two men nodded curtly to each other as I did an about-face and took the car back to Curran's Motors on Tenth Avenue between Thirty-Fifth and Thirty-Sixth Streets, where we had garaged our automobiles for years.

When I got back home and used my key to open the front door, the office was vacant and I could hear muffled voices from the kitchen. Presumably, Wolfe, Fritz, and Farber were huddling and working out the transition. Here was a meeting I was happy to avoid.

I dropped into my chair in the office and was cleaning my typewriter with the little brush that came with it when Wolfe walked in carrying a frosted stein full of beer and went to sit in the reinforced chair at his desk built to accommodate his seventh of a ton. "How are the boys getting along in there?" I asked, tilting my head in the direction of the kitchen.

He raised his shoulders half an inch and dropped them, his version of a shrug. "Mr. Farber appears to be competent," he answered in a tone that suggested some doubt.

"Well, I know you will generously share with him your vast culinary knowledge, and one can only hope that he will behave accordingly and heed your golden words of wisdom."

"Archie, shut up."

"Yes, sir." I then filled Wolfe in on Fritz's travel plans and our upcoming trip to the airport. "I have told him to cable us on his arrival in Geneva and let us know how and where he can be reached while he's there."

Wolfe shuddered. For him, any ride in an airplane was a reckless and foolhardy venture. He had a similar feeling about riding in automobiles, although he had become almost used to the occasional venture to the barbershop, the Metropolitan Orchid Show, or the Long Island home of fellow orchid fancier Lewis Hewitt, where he dined yearly.

But on those forays, he insisted I be the driver. However, even with me behind the wheel, he would sit on the edge of the seat and hold the specially installed hand grip in our Heron sedan with white knuckles. And he was quick to comment when he thought I was driving too fast, which was much of the time.

"Does Fritz know anyone other than his cousin in Geneva?" Wolfe asked. I'm always surprised at how little Wolfe knows about Fritz and his life, given how much time they spend together in the kitchen, planning meals and sometimes arguing over specific ingredients and proportions.

"When we head for the airport, I'll find out everything I can," I said, answering his question. "I don't like to see him leaving any more than you do, but I don't feel we have a choice. Just look at what he's been like the last few weeks. He may still be delivering fine meals to us, but you can tell his heart isn't in it."

Wolfe grimly nodded his agreement and picked up an orchid catalog that came in the mail. The discussion was ended.

Fritz had packed efficiently, which did not surprise me. I loaded his suitcase and carry-on into the Heron's trunk and we were off to the Idlewild Airport in Queens.

"How long has it been since you were in Geneva?" I asked.

"Oh, Archie, it has been so many years now. That was when my aunt Celine died. My parents both passed away when I was just a boy, as I believe you know, and she reared me. A very kind lady. She was like a mother and she treated me just like her own son, Paul." At the mention of the man he was going to Switzerland to search for, Fritz sighed.

"Now that you mention it, I do remember that trip you made. For the whole time you were gone, it was a little over a week, Mr. Wolfe and I ate every night at Rusterman's. The meals were fine, but not as good as yours."

"Thank you, Archie. I am sorry to be leaving both of you for . . . well, for a while."

"This is something you need to do," I told him. "Besides, Paul, who else do you still know in Geneva?"

"There is Émile Maillard, who I met at school and who I then worked with in my first restaurant job."

"Tell me about that job."

Fritz sighed again. "It was called Armond's, after the owner. Small, only a few tables, but with a very loyal clientele. After an apprenticeship, I became a sous-chef and Émile was in charge of the pastries. It was a good way to get started in the business and

Armond—his last name was Laurent—was almost like a father to both of us. I recall those days fondly."

"What does Émile Maillard do now?"

"He has his own restaurant, called Émile's, of course. I was there only once, when I went back for my aunt's funeral. It was very popular and I am sure it still is."

"Have you stayed in touch with Maillard?"

"We exchange Christmas cards and the occasional letter. He had been married for many years, but his wife died a few months ago. He has children and grandchildren, as well."

"I'm sure you will see him on this trip then, right?"

"Oh yes, I will call him when I arrive in Geneva. And he also has been very close to Paul over the years. I believe Paul helped Émile financially when he opened his restaurant."

"Will you see anyone else?"

"I don't know that yet. I have been away for so long that other than Émile, I am not sure who I would still know. Several of my friends from the past have died, which I have learned from Paul's letters, and others may have moved away."

"Fritz, it is important that when you get settled, send us a telegram about how we can reach you. Also, you can telephone anytime and reverse the charges. Mr. Wolfe is most insistent about that."

"I do not want to take advantage of his generosity, Archie."

"He feels it is very important that we keep in close touch with you and I agree."

"I am sorry to be leaving him—and you. I hope Mr. Farber will prove to be satisfactory."

"I don't want you worrying about that right now, Fritz. You will have plenty to occupy you in Geneva and I join Mr. Wolfe in the hope that you will locate your cousin," I said as we pulled into the airport parking lot.

"Thank you, Archie. You don't have to come in with me."

"Please indulge me, Fritz. I have learned that things have a way of going wrong in airports and we need to make sure that the airline has not somehow dropped the ball."

Fritz nodded his acceptance and we went into the terminal with me toting his bags.

"I can carry those, Archie," he insisted.

"You will have plenty of opportunity to carry them before this trip in over," I insisted back. "Take advantage of my good nature."

Fortunately, everything went smoothly at the airline counter and Fritz was able to pay his fare and get his suitcase checked. I then walked him to the gate and waited until he and the other passengers lined up to go to the tarmac and board.

"Thank you so much, Archie," he said. "I am afraid that I have taken you away from your work."

"Mr. Wolfe can do without me for a while," I told him. "We wouldn't want to spoil him, would we?"

Fritz nodded, swallowing hard, tried to smile, and began following the other passengers as they shuffled toward the boarding door. I wondered when I would see him again.

CHAPTER 4

Life in the brownstone went on without Fritz. Wolfe continued to spend four hours a day, nine to eleven in the morning and four to six in the afternoon, up in the plant rooms with his orchid nurse, Theodore Horstmann, as they babied the ten thousand varieties of what Wolfe referred to as his "concubines."

Leon Farber seemed to be hard at work and his first dinner, squabs with sausage and sauerkraut, was adequate and maybe even as good as if Fritz had prepared it. Wolfe appeared to be satisfied, although earlier in the day when I was in the office, I could hear voices being raised in the kitchen. I wisely kept my distance.

In the meantime, the bank balance received a welcome injection when Wolfe, with my assistance, nailed an embezzler who had been skimming funds from a chain of furniture stores in New Jersey. The guilty party was an in-house accountant who happened to be the nephew of the chain's owner.

Said owner at first refused to believe a close relative could have betrayed his trust but we were able to provide damning evidence that the young man did indeed put self before family. It was not a pretty sight when I got the two men together in Wolfe's office and watched the accountant crumble in tears while his uncle seethed and finally began screaming in frustration.

Wolfe, who can't stand scenes, marched out and left me to receive a check for the agreed-upon fee from our client, who was in a state of devastation.

Fritz had been gone for more than two days when we got a call from him one morning just after Wolfe had descended by elevator from the plant rooms. I accepted the charges from the operator as Wolfe picked up his phone.

"Fritz, how are you?" I asked.

"All right," came the response from what was a surprisingly good international connection. "I am staying at the home of Émile Maillard, who I mentioned to you, Archie." He then gave us the telephone number.

"Any news of your cousin?" Wolfe posed.

"Not yet, sir. I have talked to some of the people who know him, but they all tell me they haven't seen him for days, maybe even weeks, and they don't understand what could have happened to him. No one I spoke to, including of course Émile, said that Paul had seemed worried or was acting strangely the last time they saw him."

"Have you gone to the police?"

"Yes, I have, Mr. Wolfe, and they told me as they had told Mr. Hitchcock that there had been no recent cases of missing persons and no bodies have been pulled from the lake in almost a year."

"What do you plan to do next?"

"I am going first thing in the morning to the steamship office. I know that Mr. Hitchcock from London already went there but maybe I can find someone working for the company that I knew years ago. Geneva is still a small town and, being here once again, I see that it has changed very little since my last visit."

"Please report again, Fritz, in the next day or no more than two," Wolfe said. Fritz promised he would and the connection was ended.

"It doesn't sound good," I said, swiveling to face Wolfe.

He grunted. "Would it make sense to send Saul to Geneva?" He was referring to Saul Panzer, the freelance operative we often used who is the best in the business at holding a tail or tracking someone who doesn't want to be found.

"I suppose it would be okay if you don't care how much dough we spend, but I can't see that, good as he is, Saul would have much luck in a place where he doesn't know the lay of the land. Fritz has the advantage of knowing people and speaking their language, both literally and figuratively."

Wolfe's scowl tacitly acknowledged his agreement. "Very well, we wait, at least for a while. I was in Geneva once, many years ago, and I concur with Fritz that in many ways it is indeed a small city, albeit one that has played an outsized role in international affairs. Did you know that it had been the headquarters of the League of Nations?"

"The operation that went kaput after World War I when the United States refused to join?"

"Archie, although your knowledge of world history is shaky at best, in this instance you are essentially correct."

"Well, even a stopped clock is right twice a day."

Wolfe glowered at me but did not deign to respond, turning instead to his new book, *The Renaissance*, by Will Durant.

"Before you get too far into that fat book that was delivered this morning by Murger's Books, I'd like to know how you feel that our new chef is working out."

"Adequate, at least as a temporary expediency. Why do you ask?"

"I don't much care for the guy's attitude. He doesn't like the idea of having to serve me breakfast. Oh, he does do it, all right, but he refuses to say more than a few words and he sniffs a lot, as though it's an effort for him. I get the impression he feels it's beneath him to have to wait on me, a mere underling. How does he do with your breakfast?"

"Again, adequate. And he of course realizes that as executor I have a great deal to say about the management and operation of Rusterman's."

"Good point. He does not want word to get back to Felix that he is displeasing the restaurant's benefactor. He might then end up finding himself flipping flapjacks and frying eggs in a greasy spoon tucked under the elevated tracks on Third Avenue."

Wolfe's cheeks creased, his version of a smile. It was pleasing to know that I could still amuse him on occasion. That helps to at least partially offset the times I rile him up.

But then, part of my job has always been to get under Wolfe's skin. When he hired me back in the dark ages, he said he expected me to be a burr under his saddle (my words, not his) and to spur him to action. So this I try to do, with limited success. Wolfe can be lazy, as he freely admits, and getting him to keep focused on the job at hand can be a challenge and one that I accept. But that doesn't mean that it's fun.

CHAPTER 5

The next two days passed uneventfully and with no word from Fritz. On the third morning I sat in the office typing correspondence Wolfe had dictated the day before and thinking I should call Geneva to check on our traveler. But just as I contemplated making an international call, the telephone rang.

"Nero Wolfe's office, Archie Goodwin speaking," I answered as I invariably do.

The first voice I heard was that of an operator informing me that a call was coming through from Switzerland. "Do you accept the charges," she asked crisply, and I responded in the affirmative.

A bit of static ensued and then came a male voice in broken but understandable English. "Is this the residence of Mr. Nero Wolfe?"

"Yes, it is. I am Archie Goodwin. Who is calling?"

"Oh, Mr. Goodwin, of course I know your name from Fritz. I am Émile Maillard. Perhaps you have heard of me?"

"I have, Mr. Maillard."

"Yes, good. I am calling you and Mr. Nero Wolfe because I am worried about Fritz."

"Go on," I said, my mouth suddenly as dry as the Sahara.

"As I know you are aware, Mr. Goodwin, Fritz has been staying with me since he arrived in Geneva and I was delighted to be his host. But now . . ."

"But now, *what*?" I barked, gripping the receiver with a stranglehold.

"But now," Maillard continued, "he is gone."

"What do you mean, *gone*?"

"When I arose this morning, I realized that Fritz had not slept in his bed last night. I asked neighbors and no one had seen him. I then went to the pier where he had been searching for his cousin Paul, and nobody there had seen him, either."

"Had Fritz talked to you about his plans for today?"

"He told me yesterday afternoon that he was going to meet with someone today who knew where his cousin was. His clothing appears to be intact, although I don't know how much he brought with him."

"Did he give you the name of that person?"

"No, Mr. Goodwin. I asked him but he would not tell me, for what reason I do not know."

"Mr. Maillard, please call this number again if you learn anything about Fritz. And you can reverse the charges again, please. Also, we may be calling you as well."

"That is fine. I am a widower and retired, so I am home much of the time, although I occasionally serve as maître d' at my restaurant."

When Wolfe came down from the plant rooms at eleven and buzzed for beer, I filled him in on the call from Maillard.

"If we don't hear from Fritz or Mr. Maillard by this time tomorrow, telephone Maillard again."

"Aren't you getting worried?"

"Confound it, yes! I am worried. But as Abraham Lincoln said to one of his generals, a man named Hooker, 'Beware of rashness.'"

"Well, we certainly wouldn't want to be rash, would we?"

"Archie, as I have said before, you lack patience and my exercise of it infuriates you. I remain confident of Fritz's ability to fend for himself. Besides, what would you have me do?"

He had me there. There wasn't a lot we could do without some help from people in Geneva and, so far, that was not forthcoming.

Wolfe was right about at least one thing: I tend to lack patience and get frustrated when I can't make things happen. For the rest of the day, I tried to find ways to keep busy and take my mind off Switzerland. Fortunately, I had a date that night with Lily Rowan to see a new musical comedy on Broadway that was getting good reviews.

For those of you who are new to these narratives, a few words about Lily: I have known her well, make that *very* well, since an afternoon years ago in Upstate New York when a bull charged me in a meadow and, to escape it, I leaped over a fence and landed with a thud on my rear end.

A lovely honey-blonde young woman wearing a yellow shirt and slacks clapped and chirped, "Beautiful, Escamillo. Do it again!" This was Lily. And Escamillo, which she has called me ever since, is a toreador in the opera *Carmen*.*

Lily is wealthy, through the inheritance from her late father, an Irish immigrant who made his fortune by building many of the sewers that still undergird the streets of New York.

---

* *Some Buried Caesar* by Rex Stout, 1938

Lily also likes to say that she is lazy, but I strongly dispute that claim. For as long as I have known her, she has given generously to causes ranging from orphanages and shelters for battered women to boys' clubs and food pantries. She heads up a group of like-minded women who meet annually at her vacation retreat up in Katonah to plan ways of helping the underprivileged and abused.

Lily lives in a duplex penthouse in Midtown Manhattan that has been the subject of articles in home design magazines. She throws elaborate parties here, many of them to benefit one or more of the charities she supports. Her guests at these parties long ago learned to bring their checkbooks with them.

When she is not otherwise occupied with her many projects, chances are you might see us together at the opera, a Rangers hockey game at the Garden, or dancing in the ballroom of the Churchill Hotel, where we have been known to cut a mean tango. And it is important for me to tell you that wherever we go, I foot the bill. And Lily never argues about that.

After the musical, which both of us enjoyed, we had a late supper at Rusterman's, where Felix thoughtfully placed us at a table nestled in a quiet corner. "Escamillo, all evening you have asked me questions about what I have been up to and now it's my turn: Do you and Wolfe have any cases you can tell me about? You live such an exciting life."

"Not always as exciting as you may think, my love. May I unburden myself to you?"

"But of course. I like to think I am something more than just an escort for a handsome and debonair gentleman."

"You are far more than an escort. You are, well . . . among many other things, a confidant."

"Ooh, I like that. Confidant sounds so . . . so *confidential*. So secretive. I am ready for you to unburden yourself."

"Okay, here goes," I said and proceeded to tell her all about Fritz's venture to Geneva, his subsequent disappearance, and my unease.

"Oh dear. It seems to me that you have good reason to be concerned," Lily said. "I know Fritz well enough, I think, to realize he is not the type to seek out trouble. But I suppose it is possible that trouble has sought *him* out for some reason."

"That's certainly been on my mind. Wolfe outwardly seems less concerned than I am, but I believe he's more worried than he lets on."

Lily chuckled. "Your boss does not exactly go overboard with his emotions, does he?"

I laughed with her. "No, he holds things in pretty well. When he is really irate, he has been known to cut loose with 'Pah,' 'Egad,' or even 'Great Hounds and Cerberus!'"

"And what do you say or do when you get angry, Archie?" Lily asked with a twinkle in her eye. "You never seem angry to me."

"Maybe Wolfe over the years has taught me how to hold it in," I told her. "And for some reason, I've never been much for swearing. Maybe it was because my parents never used foul language and they didn't expect their children to, either. You could say they led by example."

"Now that you mention it, I don't think I ever heard my mother or father curse, either, although I may have given them reason to, especially as a teen."

"I don't believe that for a minute. I believe you were born wearing a halo."

Now that brought a roar from Lily. "Oh, Escamillo, what a fraud I am. How ever have I been able to fool you for so long?"

"Maybe it's the way you bat those eyelashes. I'm a sucker for that."

"Now that I know, I'm going to run out and buy some super-long lashes. You won't stand a chance when I'm done with you."

"My dear, I already don't stand a chance, as I think you are aware. Oh and one more thing: I was more than a little depressed when the evening started, but being with you has brightened me more than I can tell you."

"Tell me anyway, Archie. I love to hear you talk like this. You're quite a glib guy, you know."

"Aw shucks, little lady, how you do go on with all that molasses. It makes a feller go all weak in the knees when you talk that way."

"Let's get serious for a minute," Lily said. "I know you're concerned about Fritz, and it sounds like with good reason. Do you think you might have to go to Switzerland?"

"I really don't know. And the bigger question is, if I do go, will Wolfe go as well?"

"That would really boggle the mind, to use a phrase that's been going around a lot recently."

"Well, he and I did travel to Montenegro, as you recall. So . . . I suppose anything's possible."

CHAPTER 6

The next morning after breakfast, I sat in the office with coffee, willing the telephone to ring. But it stayed stubbornly silent, and it remained mute until Wolfe came down from the plant rooms, then we would be placing a call to Émile Maillard in Geneva.

When Wolfe did descend by elevator at eleven, he broke a morning ritual and instead of asking if I had slept well, he said "Have there been any calls?"

After I shook my head, he buzzed for beer. It was promptly brought in by Leon Farber, who, after setting the two bottles and a stein on the desk, turned to glower at me. "Same to you, fella," I thought.

"Please telephone Mr. Maillard," Wolfe ordered, and I started the process of placing the international call, which took about three minutes, during which Wolfe picked up his receiver.

"Allo," came the voice of Maillard amid some static.

"Hello, sir, this is Nero Wolfe."

"Yes, Mr. Wolfe."

"Do you have any news concerning Fritz Brenner?"

"I have heard nothing at all, Mr. Wolfe, not a word."

"Have you talked to the police again?"

"I did, yesterday afternoon, and they said they still had no information about either Fritz or Paul Berard. They have grown tired of me coming to them asking questions."

"Although their jobs are often challenging, the police can be difficult to deal with," Wolfe told him, and I stifled a smile as I thought about the bombastic Homicide Inspector Lionel T. Cramer and his pugnacious sidekick, Sergeant Purley Stebbins of the New York City Police Department. Not to mention Leutenant George Rowcliff, about whom the less said the better.

"I am sorry I do not have any information for you, Mr. Wolfe. I am very frustrated and also sad."

"An understandable feeling, sir. Please telephone us if you learn anything." Maillard assured us he would and the call was ended.

"I am going to Geneva," I told Wolfe after several seconds of silence between us. "If you feel I am deserting you, I offer my resignation."

"There is no need for that, Archie. We will go together."

I was stunned. Of course we had left the brownstone before to go to Montenegro, but when Lily asked me if Wolfe and I would go to Switzerland and I replied that "anything's possible," I really thought the odds were slim for such a venture. Those odds had now drastically changed and I was faced with what would be a series of logistical challenges.

First off, what to do about Wolfe's prized ten thousand orchids in the three climate-controlled room in the roof-top greenhouse? Theodore Horstmann, who nurtures these beauties like a mother hen, could stay on, of course, in his small bedroom adjoining the greenhouse. But who would feed him?

Since we already had Leon Farber, he could come in every day and prepare Theodore's meals. And what about the office and the mail?

The only time Wolfe and I had traveled overseas together, Saul Panzer stayed in a spare bedroom and handled the telephone calls, the bills, the deliveries, and the rest of the brownstone's business operations while still being able to operate his own thriving operation as a private investigator.

As for passports, both Wolfe's and mine were valid as they would be for years to come. That left the travel arrangements, which of course fell to me, as Wolfe is loath to trouble himself with such mundane details. Before long, I would be on the phone with Larry Marks, the travel agent who only days ago set up Fritz's flight to Geneva.

A call to Saul Panzer quickly confirmed that he was willing to dwell in the brownstone and oversee its operations in our absence. "Sorry to hear about what's going on with Fritz," he said after I had explained the situation. "I'll do whatever I can to keep things operating at this end, Archie."

"I have no doubt whatever of that. Fritz's replacement in the kitchen, the dour Leon Farber, who comes from Rusterman's, can't hold a spatula to Fritz, but he's adequate. Feel free to make recommendations about what you would like on your plate. Also, Theodore will be having his meals in the brownstone as usual, but not in the dining room, also as usual. He eats in the kitchen, so you will have the dining room to yourself in regal splendor."

"Regal splendor, eh? I like that. Can I also assume that I will have free rein when it comes to the liquor cart in the office?"

"Be my guest—rather, Mr. Wolfe's. He might, however, draw

the line at you going to the wine cellar and helping yourself to a bottle of Remisier cognac."

"Heaven forbid that should happen," Saul said in a faux shocked tone. "I happen to know your boss reserves that nectar for special guests and special occasions. Although I frankly admit to being jealous that our old newspaper pal and fellow poker player, Lon Cohen, gets to drink that whenever he dines in the brownstone."

He was referring to Lon Cohen of the *New York Gazette*, America's fifth-largest newspaper.

"The difference between you and Lon is that he often supplies us with information from his sources that's helpful in a case we're working on."

"Yeah, but look how you repay him by feeding him and his paper scoops, so it's hardly a case of you being beholden to the man."

"Look, here is what I will do for you: The next time you have dinner with us at the brownstone, I will suggest to Wolfe that it might be a nice idea to break out the Remisier. I will say to him, 'Saul has always heard about how great that brandy is and it might be good to have him sample it and find out for himself.'"

"Now, Archie, I wouldn't want to put you out on my account."

"Anything for a friend," I replied. "And as you well know, you're jake in Wolfe's estimation, so I'm sure he would uncork a bottle. Just don't do any uncorking yourself in our absence."

"As if I would," Saul sniffed, trying without success to appear hurt.

"Enough of this bantering," I said. "Are you working on any cases right now?"

"Yeah and this one's a doozy. A fortyish woman in Flatbush thinks her husband is a Communist and she hired me to tail him and find out where he's been going lately at night. He clams up when she asks him about it."

"What makes her think the guy is a Red?"

"She found some Commie literature in one of his pants pockets when she took his suit to the cleaners."

"Maybe he just picked it up from somebody passing stuff out on the street. The other day, a woman on Lexington tried to hand me a booklet titled *The Exploitation of the Proletariat*. I told her thanks, but no thanks."

"I suppose your scenario is possible," Saul conceded.

"Or, it could be her husband is having an affair."

"That occurred to me as well, but from the pics of him she showed me, he doesn't look at all like the type."

"It's those joes who don't look like the type that often turn out to *be* the type," I said.

"It was just a thought," Saul said. "The wife doesn't seem like a crackpot and things have been some slow of late, so I'm taking her seriously. But that's all I have going on right now."

Within seconds after I hung up with Saul, the phone squawked. It was Larry Marks, from the travel agency.

"Hi, Archie. Pending your approval, I've got you and Mr. Wolfe on a flight to London in the evening day after tomorrow." He gave me the airline and departure time, which I took down. "Now, Archie," he continued, "I took the liberty of booking you both in first class, given Mr. Wolfe's . . ."

"Size," I completed his sentence. "That is an absolute necessity," I assured him.

"Just so you know, "Larry said, "the flight includes a stopover for refueling in Gander, Newfoundland, which may mean more than an hour on the ground. Also, after you land at Heathrow, there will be a two-hour delay before the departure for Geneva. That is the best we could do, given what's available."

"I will confirm everything with Mr. Wolfe and get back to you. Anything else I need to know?"

"Not really," Larry said. "When you give me the go-ahead, the agency will pay for the tickets and bill you." I thanked him, checking another item off my "things to do before leaving" list and then turned to Wolfe.

"We've got our flights for two days from now," I told him. "On the way to London, we have a long stopover at Gander, in the middle of nowhere, which you may remember from our trip to Montenegro."

He made a noise that, roughly translated, was "Grrr."

"Yeah, I totally agree. But these damned planes can only carry so much fuel and, just like cars, they need filling stations. Larry Marks also says we have a two-hour layover in England before our flight to Switzerland takes off."

Wolfe scowled at me, picked up his book, and hid behind it.

"Hey, don't shoot the messenger. I thought it was important for you to be in full possession of the details of our trip so you're not surprised later. And I've lost count of the number of times that you've told me that you don't like surprises."

I received no answer, nor did I expect one.

Wolfe stewed for several hours, but once he got used to the idea that he would be wedged into airplane seats for many hours with two extensive on-the-ground gaps between legs of our trek, he reconciled himself to reality. In fact, he was almost—but not quite—gregarious at dinner that night as we consumed veal birds in casserole, adequately prepared by our fill-in chef.

Wolfe always sets the subject of the dinner-table conversation and this time it was the future of the new medium of television and the impact it could have on family dynamics.

"Archie, I have read that sales of what are called 'TV trays' have increased rapidly, along with the popularity of so-called television dinners, developed a few years ago by a man named Thomas. These come in plastic-encased packages and can quickly be heated in the oven. This allows families to sit around their living room eating and watching television programs on a piece of furniture that becomes the room's focal point," he said with a shudder.

"I can't imagine that ever gaining popularity," I said.

"One can only hope you are correct. The idea that home life would revolve around a television programming schedule is reprehensible."

We went on to imagine a world in which having more than one television set in the home might split up the family and all but destroy the tradition of the family dinner at the dining room or kitchen table.

After we finished the meal, we retired to the office with coffee and turned our thoughts to the upcoming trip.

"Have you given any thought to where we will stay in Geneva?" I asked Wolfe.

"You seem to place a good deal of trust in Mr. Marks. He likely will have recommendations. First, the lodgings must be centrally located. I require a room with a king-size bed and a commodious chair, with a floor lamp. And, of course, a bathroom *en suite*. I assume the better hotels in so cosmopolitan a city must have elevators, but it is worth confirming. And perhaps he can recommend some nearby restaurants."

"Seems likely. I will pass your requests along to Larry, along with my own. Anything else?"

"Not at the moment," he said, turning to his book and buzzing for beer. He hates to be bothered with details, but if there is a slip-up of any kind, I will be the one who gets the blame, count on it.

* * *

The next morning after breakfast, I was parked at my desk in the office with coffee as usual when the phone rang, a call from Switzerland. My hope that it was Fritz got quickly dashed when, after the operator put the call through, I heard the voice of Émile Maillard.

"Allo, Mr. Wolfe. Or is it Mr. Goodwin?"

"It's Archie Goodwin, Mr. Maillard. Do you have any news for us?"

"Alas, no, sir, I do not. But I thought I should telephone and bear the cost. I have heard nothing at all from or about Fritz."

"I should have asked you this earlier: Are you able to tell if Fritz took any extra clothes with him when he left your place?"

"That thought occurred to me as well, but when I looked in his room, I could not tell with any certainty. Fritz is very precise and his apparel was either hung up in the wardrobe or, with the shirts, socks, and underthings, folded neatly in the drawers. He might have taken some extra garments with him, but I do not know what he had packed. I am so sorry not to be of any help."

"Don't worry about that now. Mr. Wolfe and I will be arriving in Geneva in two days, and once we have settled into a hotel we will telephone you."

"If you do not have lodgings yet, I can highly recommend either the Hotel Lac Leman, which as you would expect by its name that it is very close to the lake, or the Helvetia, which is in the same area. People I know who have stayed at each of them have told me they are very fine."

"Thank you, I will keep that in mind," I told him as we ended the call.

Saul was to come over later in the morning to settle into the spare bedroom and meet Fritz's temporary replacement in the kitchen. For Wolfe, riding in taxis was definitely not an option, so Saul would be driving us to the airport in the Heron sedan when the time came. The trip was going to be hard enough on Wolfe, so anything at all that I could do to make things easier on him also would make things easier on me.

Less than five minutes later, Larry Marks called and what transpired was as if he had overheard my conversation with Maillard.

"Archie, I've got a couple of hotel possibilities for you: One is the Lac Leman, right on the shores of the lake, and the other is the Helvetia, less than a block away. Both get high ratings from Michelin, although based on what has been told to us by our clients," Larry said, "I would lean toward the Lac Leman, in part because of a superb restaurant, the Chez Marc, which is on the street level of the hotel."

"Let's go with that, then," I told him. "We will want adjoining or at least close-by rooms with baths, preferably on one of the lower floors. And because Wolfe wanted to know, I have to ask: Does the hotel have elevators?"

There was a momentary pause before Marks responded. "Well, of *course it does,* Archie. You don't think that I would book rooms for valued clients in walk-ups, do you?"

"Sorry, but I had to ask, Larry. That's just a part of my role here."

The travel agent responded with a slight chuckle, which it sounded like he was trying to stifle. "Archie, we should have no trouble whatever getting you those rooms, but I will confirm with a telephone call."

CHAPTER 7

The day of our departure finally had arrived. Wolfe was in his room filling his suitcase and a smaller carry-on after having spent time with Theodore Horstmann, giving him explicit instructions regarding the care and feeding of the orchids.

Now came my own packing. Among other things, one sport coat, several shirts, a couple of ties, blue jeans, a black turtleneck sweater, black knit cap, and of course my Marley .38, a shoulder holster, and boxes of ammo, all just in case. Although I was never much of a Boy Scout growing up in Ohio, I've always hewed to their motto, "Be prepared."

In mid morning, a messenger came to the brownstone with a packet from Larry Marks. It included our airline tickets, reservations at the Hotel Lac Leman, and an invoice. I wrote a check to the travel agency and gave it to Saul Panzer to mail. Speaking of Saul, he already had made himself at home, both in his room and in the office, from which he would run his own investigative operations in our absence.

Two hours before our scheduled departure, Saul eased the Heron to the curb in front of the brownstone. Anyone passing by on our West Thirty-Fifth Street block that afternoon would have been treated to the sight of Nero Wolfe coming down the seven steps to the sidewalk clad in a felt pirate hat, a gray overcoat with a fur collar, a scarf wrapped twice around his neck, and black gloves. He carried a red thorn walking stick, which I've always felt was a bit showy, given that despite his bulk, Wolfe is remarkably nimble and sure-footed. But then, there is no explaining eccentricity.

Once inside the sedan's back seat, Wolfe gripped the hand strap as though it were a lifeline and wore a grim expression. This despite the fact that Saul was his second-most trusted driver (after me). We slid smoothly into traffic and were on our way to the Idlewild Airport in Queens.

There is little to report concerning our passage through the airport. Everything went smoothly, both at the ticket counter and in the boarding process. Wolfe, still grim-faced, settled into the first-class window seat that was able, albeit barely, to accommodate his dimensions.

From the small carry-on bag he was toting, Wolfe pulled out one of the books he had brought along for company, while I, in the aisle seat next to his, settled in with a copy of *Time* magazine, which had been handed to me by a smiling and beautifully coiffed stewardess, whose shiny high-heeled pumps complemented well-shaped legs. Okay, so I admit to having snuck a peek as she moved smoothly along the aisle. If that is defined as lechery, I plead guilty.

The takeoff was smooth, although Wolfe grimaced and kept his eyes tightly closed until well after we had left the ground, gone airborne, and finally leveled off. About an hour into the flight, we were served drinks and my seatmate was pleased to see that Remmers beer was on the menu. I had scotch and water, which was welcome after the tensions of the day, brought on in large part by Wolfe's own anxieties.

Dinner menus were passed out and I chose the filet mignon while Wolfe opted for Dover sole. I thought my meal was okay, although when I looked over at Wolfe, he wore a frown. Once you have been consistently fed by Fritz Brenner, all else pales in comparison.

The droning of the plane's propellors must have put me to sleep because I jerked awake when the announcement came that we would be landing at Gander Airport in Newfoundland for the refueling. We were told we would be on the ground for more than an hour. I looked over at Wolfe who was dozing and showed no signs of awakening.

I needed to stretch my legs, so when we had settled on the Gander tarmac and the engines wheezed to a stop, I filed off the aircraft with at least two dozen other passengers and walked into the terminal. The hall was surprisingly large, although architecturally unimpressive. If pressed to name its style, I would have called it modernist, or possibly bland. But then, an airport is meant to be functional, nothing more.

I wandered around for a few minutes, bought a Canadian magazine titled *MacLean's*, and then went back to the plane, where Wolfe was still asleep.

Wolfe didn't stir as we took off again. I paged through *MacLean's*, which seemed like a Canadian version of *Time* or *Newsweek*, and read an article predicting that in the years ahead, Toronto would surpass Montreal as the country's largest city.

I had no horse in that race but, a few years back, Lily and I had spent a couple of leisurely days in Toronto, mainly to see a musical comedy in which a close friend of hers got cast as a night-club singer. The city seemed quiet and staid given its size, but also remarkably clean, especially when compared to New York.

I fell asleep again over the mid-Atlantic but was jarred awake by Wolfe, who needed to use the facilities. I got up and slid out of my seat, wondering how he would fit through the narrow toilet door. He did, with relative ease, and when he returned with me still standing in the aisle, he gave me a glower that puzzled me. Maybe in his overall discomfort, he merely took it out on the person closest to him.

I just shrugged and tried to fall asleep again as he resumed reading. He asked for another Remmers, brought to him by the winsome stewardess. As she leaned across me to serve him both the beer bottle and a glass, she winked at me and I returned the wink before dropping off again.

I awoke sometime later to the aroma of coffee and the bustle of the cabin crew as they set about serving what passed for breakfast at twenty-thousand feet. The quality of the meal was easy to criticize, but given that it had to be prepared in the tight quarters of an airplane galley, I tended to be generous with my criticism. However, Wolfe had no such compunctions and he screwed up his face as the tray with scrambled eggs, bacon, juice, and toast was set on his drop-down table.

But he soldiered on, manfully overcoming any culinary distaste he harbored. He polished off the contents of the tray and asked for another helping, which he got. Ah, the benefits of flying in the first-class cabin.

After the remnants of the meal had efficiently been cleared away, we got word over the intercom that we were preparing to touch down at London's Heathrow Airport. The landing was somewhat bumpy, but even Wolfe seemed unfazed as we taxied toward the terminal.

Once inside the terminal, we had almost two hours hour to kill before our flight to Geneva was scheduled to depart. Wolfe dubiously considered the size of the chairs in the boarding area. He finally wedged himself into one of them, opened his book, and buried his nose in it while I went to the airline desk to check us in on the Geneva plane.

This was a smaller aircraft—only two engines—than the one in which we had crossed the Atlantic and once again we were booked into the first-class cabin. Wolfe eased his way into the window seat with a minimum of fuss while I was next to him on the aisle, as before.

Once during our flight, I craned my neck and, looking past Wolfe and out the window, saw that we were passing over snow-covered mountains. My brief view was a spectacular one, but it was lost on Wolfe, who preferred his book to the postcard picture Alps below him.

We were served a light lunch, sandwich and a salad, and then, as the pilot informed us, we began our descent into Geneva. The landing was far smoother than the one at Heathrow and before long we were filing out of the plane, down the outdoor steps to the tarmac, and into the terminal. The air had a fresh smell, the sky was blue, and, during our short walk, I noted that mountains were visible in all directions.

I retrieved our luggage and, with Wolfe two steps behind me, we went outside and were quickly able to get a cab from the waiting line. "The Lac Leman Hotel," I said to the driver, getting a "Yes, governor," in reply, reminding me of cab drivers Lily and I had when we were in London. When we pulled from the curb and accelerated, Wolfe searched for a nonexistent hand grab.

I had thought Toronto was a clean city, but this town was the winner in that competition, hands down. The buildings seemed to cap off at five or six stories, with no skyscrapers in sight, only church spires. Trees and flowers lined many of the streets and also the banks of the river, which, as I was to learn, was the Rhone. Grim-faced, Wolfe sat silent until he saw a long and impressive white and columned structure that dominated a grassy hillside.

"That, Archie, is the Palace of Nations, which was the headquarters of the League of Nations until World War Two and which now holds many departments of the United Nations."

"At least when that old League folded, they were able to find a new use for it," I observed. Several minutes later, our cab pulled up in front of a five-story stone building. It faced a tree-lined boulevard that followed the shoreline of the body of water I will henceforth refer to in this narrative as Lake Geneva, despite the fact that the Swiss and French call it Lac Leman.

"This is the fine Hotel Lac Leman, gents," the cabbie said in either an English accent or a reasonable facsimile thereof.

I paid the man in Swiss Francs from the bills and coins I had gotten at the *bureau de change* in the Geneva airport. My tip must have pleased him, because he gave me a broad smile and a nod as a uniformed young bellhop unloaded our luggage from the taxi's trunk.

The hotel's lobby was small but elegant, exuding a "yes, this is a pricey place and don't you forget it" aura. A tall, lean, silver-haired man with a thin mustache and clad in a perfectly tailored navy-blue pin-striped suit greeted us at the check-in counter with a smile that appeared to be genuine. "Gentlemen, welcome to the Lac Leman. We are here to serve you in every way we are able."

And to relieve us of our money, I thought as I handed him our reservations. "Ah, yes, two Imperial rooms, second floor," he said, nodding curtly to the waiting bellhop and giving him the keys to both rooms.

Wolfe remained silent as we went up in the elevator with the boy and our bags. "Have you stayed with us before?" he asked in accented but understandable English.

"Nope, first time," I said. "I understand you have a restaurant here."

"Oh yes, we do—Chez Marc, the best in all of Geneva. It is just off the lobby. I can make a reservation for you if you like," he said.

"Thank you, we will consider it," I told him as he unlocked the door to Wolfe's room and carried his bag in. I waited in the hall until he had shown Wolfe around his new quarters.

He then went along the hall to the next door, entering with my bag and a flourish. "Here you are, sir: wardrobe in the corner as you can see, next to the bathroom, and with a window that looks out on the lake. A wonderful view, the best in Geneva. Also, we have twenty-four hour room service and, in addition to Chez Marc, there is a coffee shop just off the lobby."

He would have gone on describing both the room's and the hotel's amenities had I not handed him some coins. In my rush to get dollars swapped for francs at the Geneva airport, I had not calculated the exchange rate and had overtipped our cabbie, which surely accounted for his ear-to-ear grin. I was somewhat less liberal with my gratuity to the bellhop, although he seemed satisfied and departed with a snappy salute and a slight bow.

My room was comfortable, good-sized, and well decorated, although terming it "Imperial" was an overstatement. I went out and down the hall, knocking on Wolfe's door.

"Come in," he gruffed.

"Everything meet with your approval?" I asked, surveying the room, which was similar to my own.

"Adequate."

"More than adequate, I would say. After all, you got your king-size bed, your large and well-padded easy chair with a lamp, a desk, two other comfortable chairs, a sofa, a coffee table, and a view of the lake that the bellhop assured me was the best in all of the city of Geneva."

Unimpressed, he looked at the telephone on his bedside table. "Call Mr. Maillard; we need to meet. I will talk to him."

"Aye, aye, sir," I replied, reaching into a breast pocket for my notebook. I got Maillard's number and called the front desk, asking to be put through. After three rings, our man answered.

"Hello, sir. This is Archie Goodwin. We are in Geneva, at the Hotel Lac Leman. Mr. Wolfe is on the line." I handed him the receiver as he sat on the bed.

"Mr. Maillard, if you are able to spare some time for us, we would like to meet with you as soon as possible."

"I am only occasionally at the restaurant these days and it runs very nicely without me most of the time, so I am usually available. I can come to your hotel if that is agreeable."

"It is," Wolfe said, giving him the room number and ending the call. "Archie, please get room service to bring up coffee and croissants for three."

The coffee and rolls came a minute or so before Émile Maillard arrived. He looked to be about Fritz's age and was lean, with thinning white hair, a long face, and rimless glasses. Wolfe, who rarely stands when a visitor enters his office at home, did not hesitate to rise in this case. "Mr. Maillard, I am Nero Wolfe. Thank you for coming. And this is Mr. Goodwin." Wolfe did not go so far as to shake hands, but I did and Maillard's grip was firm.

"It is a pleasure to meet both of you," Maillard said with a smile, his English good and his manner formal and respectful.

"Please sit down, sir, we have much to talk about," Wolfe said, gesturing to one of the two chairs that flanked the sofa.

After placing the tray with the pot, cream, sugar, cups, and croissants on the coffee table, I offered to pour and both Maillard and Wolfe had coffee. After I did the honors and passed around the rolls, I took the remaining chair.

Wolfe, whose own chair faced us, set down his cup and cleared his throat. "Mr. Maillard, am I correct in assuming you have heard nothing from Mr. Brenner or Mr. Bernard since we last spoke?"

"That is correct, I am desolate to say. No word of any kind has come."

"Tell us about Mr. Bernard's work."

"He is captain of one of the steamers that takes passengers and tourists on trips over the lake. He has done this for many years now."

"What is the length of these voyages?"

"There are different trips and, at one time or another, I believe he has been a captain on them all. Some of these sailings, primarily of a sightseeing nature, stay close to Geneva and last for only an hour or two. Others are much more extensive, taking many hours and going all the way to Lausanne and Montreux. As you may know, our lake is very long—seventy kilometers—and it is partly in France, including the village of Évian-les-Bains."

"The lake boats seem to be a big business here," I put in.

"Very much so, Mr. Goodwin," Maillard said. "The longer trips carry both tourists and passengers who get on or off at stops along the way. For many who do not have automobiles, this is how they are able to move around. People who live in towns along the lake will take the boats to Geneva to shop or to work."

"In the United States, we call those commuters."

Maillard smiled and nodded. "Yes, I have heard that term before."

"How long has Mr. Bernard been a captain?" Wolfe asked.

"Oh, for many years, I think. When he was young he started out working on the boats' crews, swabbing decks and doing other menial marine chores. I do not know him nearly as well as Fritz does, but I remember Paul saying once at a party or maybe at a dinner that working on the lake had become his life's work."

"Which would seem to suggest that he enjoys his career?"

"I definitely know it to be so, Mr. Wolfe. I once was a passenger on his steamer on a short cruise that stayed close to Geneva. Friends of ours had come to Geneva from Paris on holiday and my wife and I thought they would enjoy being out on our beautiful lake. They did indeed like the experience and, after we had docked, Paul saw me from the bridge and came down to greet us on the pier. It was clear to see by his smile and his manner that he was very proud of his boat and his job as well. He said he hoped we had an enjoyable time and seemed so pleased when all of us praised the voyage. I remember him saying to me, 'Émile, for years I have urged you to ride on my boat and now you have done so and did not even tell me. Shame on you.' He wasn't really angry, of course. That is how good friends talk to each other and we are truly good friends."

"To your knowledge, has Mr. Bernard ever had difficulties relating to his job?"

Maillard shrugged. "If he has had difficulties, as you say, I have not heard of them, Mr. Wolfe. And I'm sure I would have, as friendly as we are."

"Sir, thank you for your time. It is likely that we will be speaking again."

"I am easy to locate," Maillard said, rising. "You are likely to find me either at home or, rarely, in my restaurant. As I said to you earlier, I am not really needed there much as we have a most capable and energetic young staff and I do not want to get in their way. I most often serve as the maître d' these days. No more toque for me, just a business suit.

"Oh, I almost forgot," he said, slapping his forehead. "Speaking of my restaurant, it is among the best in the city, along with Chez Marc, downstairs in this very building. It would give me great pleasure during your stay in Geneva if you would allow me to host you both as my dinner guests at Émile's. I apologize for its title," Maillard said, coloring slightly, "but my late wife insisted, saying that my name means much in culinary circles here."

"Mr. Goodwin and I would be honored to accept your invitation," Wolfe said as he got to his feet. "One favor I would ask: Can you give Mr. Goodwin directions to the dock where Mr. Bernard's vessel sailed from?"

"Of course. It is very close to here. Mr. Goodwin, if you will go down with me in the lift, I can point its location out to you from in front of the hotel."

CHAPTER 8

When we were out at the curb in front of the hotel, Maillard had me pivot to my right and he extended an arm, pointing along the shoreline. "Mr. Goodwin, the pier where many of the lake steamers depart, including the ones from the line where Paul Bernard works, is just beyond that yellow building that stands out among the white ones all around it. As you can see, it is less than two kilometers from here, an easy and very pleasant stroll."

"I assume these boats run frequently, right?"

"They do and, as I said to you and Mr. Wolfe, it is a business that employs many people. I may be showing my civic pride by saying this, but I believe the lake's steamers are famous across Europe and even beyond."

I thanked him and we chatted briefly before shaking hands. He then hailed a taxi and waved to me as he climbed in.

Back upstairs, I saw that Wolfe's door was ajar and I knocked once, getting a terse "Come in."

He sat in his chair with his book and a tall, frosted glass that looked to be filled with beer, with another bottle waiting to be opened. "I see that you have used room service," I observed.

"And they were most prompt," he said, licking his lips as he set the glass down. "This brand is tolerable, nothing more."

"I know how much this is a trial for you, given your loyalty to Remmers. What do you think of Mr. Maillard?"

"He appears to be a solid individual and it seems he has been a good friend to Paul for years. We will accept the invitation to dine at his establishment, of course."

"Of course, I never had a doubt. He showed me where the lake steamers dock," I said. "I think it would be a good idea for me to climb on one of these boats tomorrow and take it as far along the lake as possible."

Wolfe dipped his chin half an inch, his sign of approval. "Without doubt, you will be hamstrung by your inability to speak French, but your powers of observation may very likely hold you in good stead."

"Glad you think so. I'll certainly try to learn something about Paul Bernard and his whereabouts, assuming I see someone I can talk to among the boat's crew."

"English is rapidly becoming an international language, the second most-spoken tongue in the world by so many people. This growing popularity has no doubt been stimulated by the presence of great numbers of American and British Commonwealth military forces who served around the globe during the last war."

"So, you're saying that maybe, just maybe, I might find a crew member aboard one of these vessels who will understand me?"

"Archie, I have known you for more years than I care to count and I *still* don't understand you."

"Ha, ha, very funny," I shot back, but he had turned to the telephone and was asking the hotel operator for a connection. Next, I heard him speaking rapidly in French. The conversation went on for two minutes before he hung up.

"Let me guess. You were calling room service and ordering breakfast to be brought up to you tomorrow."

"Your guess is correct, as far as it goes."

"Well, this hotel has an outstanding reputation, or so we've been told. I'm sure you will be well fed in the morning. Me, I'll take my *petit déjeuner* in the coffee shop downstairs."

Wolfe set his book down, eyebrows raised. "Where did you come up with that term?"

"Did I use it correctly?"

"You did, although your pronunciation leaves something to be desired. I repeat my question."

"When I knew that we were coming to Geneva, I pulled the French-English dictionary off the shelf in the office and wrote down a bunch of words and phrases, which I then studied on the flights. By the way, I think you've got things backward this afternoon."

"How so?"

"You have already lined up your breakfast—pardon me, *petit déjeuner*—when we haven't even made plans for dinner."

Wolfe's cheeks creased. "Ah, Archie, you may now know a handful of French words and expressions, but you cannot yet follow spoken French, which is a far different challenge. I not only gave my breakfast order to the room service individual, but I also made a dinner reservation for us tonight downstairs at Chez Marc. I do hope I was not being presumptuous."

So it was that we sat in a booth in the subdued elegance of the hotel's partially filled and tastefully decorated dining room.

There, we were handed menus with a flourish by a staid and somber individual who looked like he was central casting's idea of a waiter in a deluxe restaurant.

"This will test your knowledge of French," Wolfe told me, pointing to the list of entrées.

"Believe it or not, I think I can figure most of it out. After all, the menu at Rusterman's happens to also be filled with French words and phrases, as you know all too well in your role as its overseer, and I have had years of experience ordering there, thank you very much."

After some indecision, I ended up choosing boeuf bourguignon with garlic, onions, mushrooms, and bacon, while Wolfe dined on the sole meuniére.

As we ate, he held forth on how Geneva, a relatively small city and not even the largest one in its own country, was aided by Switzerland's traditional neutrality. This national neutrality, Wolfe said, helped it to become a global center for diplomatic conferences and a headquarters city for a multitude of international institutions and organizations.

As we finishing up with coffee and crème brûlée, I asked Wolfe's opinion of his meal.

"Adequate, most adequate," he said, dabbing his lips with the napkin.

"How would you compare it to Fritz's creations?"

"His preparation of sole meunière remains unequaled."

"Which is to say that—"

"I believe I have made myself clear, Archie. Nothing more need be said on the subject."

I could only wish that Fritz had been eavesdropping upon our conversation.

CHAPTER 9

I got out of a comfortable bed at 7:30 a.m., still feeling the effects of the time difference. After showering, shaving, and getting into casual clothes and rubber-soled shoes, I walked past Wolfe's door, where he probably was consuming his delivered breakfast, much as he would have done in his bedroom at home.

The coffee shop off the lobby, like the dining room last night, was not crowded. I got ushered to a table by the window, which looked out on the lake. I saw a spout of water well offshore that was least one hundred feet high and that I later learned was one of the city's landmarks.

The meal of wheat cakes, sausage, hash brown potatoes, a fruit plate, and orange juice, served by a cheerful and rosy-cheeked young woman, was adequate, but somehow it lacked the flair of Fritz Brenner's touch, or maybe I already was feeling nostalgia for the brownstone.

I stepped outside into a sunny morning and clean, fresh air unlike what traffic-choked Manhattan had to offer most days. The walkway along a tree-lined avenue followed the sweep of the lakeshore and I felt invigorated as I picked up my pace. Approaching the pier, I saw a two-decked steamer pulling out into the lake while a similar craft coming in would soon replace it at the dock, its red-and-white Swiss flag flapping on the stern.

At the ticket window, I asked a full-faced lady with braided white hair when the next boat would depart and she responded in accented English, looking at her wristwatch. "There is a departure in twenty minutes, sir. But it is not a guided tour, if that is what you seek; this is principally to transport residents and it sails all the way to Montreux."

"That would be fine," I said, pulling out my wallet and extracting francs. "Would you like to be in the first-class lounge?" she asked.

"No, just a regular fare and a return," I said. She took cash, giving me a ticket, change, and a folder. "This will tell you where we are stopping at what you will be seeing along the route. Meals and drinks also will be served aboard."

The folder was in English, with a British Union Jack in color emblazoned on the front. I noticed that behind the ticket seller a rack held similar folders with the flags of other countries. I thanked her and turned to go, then stopped and pivoted back.

"Oh, another thing," I improvised, turning to the ticket lady. "I was in Geneva once before, on a very short trip, and ran into a man named Paul Bernard. I seem to remember that he said he was a boat captain on the lake. By chance, does he happen to work for this company?"

"Oh yes, Monsieur Bernard, he is one of our captains. But . . . hmm, I have not seen him for some time now. You could ask one of the crew members when you go aboard."

I headed up the ramp onto the twin-desk vessel with its tall smokestack and found a seat by the rail on the upper deck. The boat looked to be less than half full as we eased away from the deck and moved slowly out onto the lake in the kind of morning that chambers of commerce love. I closed my eyes and envisioned a full-color poster of a steamer in a local travel agent's window proclaiming, "Take a Relaxing Cruise on Sunny and Picturesque Lake Geneva!"

The day was indeed sunny, but I was surprised by the choppiness of the lake as we passed near the spouting fountain that I knew from my folder was called Jet d'Eau. I was becoming a regular tourist. A crew member in uniform passed by and I beckoned him. "Yes, sir," he replied with something vaguely resembling a salute.

"Do you speak English?" I asked.

"*Oui*, of course, monsieur. How may I be of help?"

I repeated my line about meeting Paul Bernard on a previous visit and wondered if he works for this fleet.

"Oh yes, he does and for many years has been one of our fine captains, but I believe that for some weeks he may have been taken ill, although I have no details."

"I am sorry to learn that," I told the sailor, who nodded curtly and headed off in the direction of the stern.

So far, I had learned nothing, other than that Bernard apparently was well thought of by his coworkers and may be ill. This trip of mine may turn out be nothing more than a fool's errand but at least I would enjoy the scenery, which included hills that sloped upward toward the snow-covered Alps, which, my folder informed me, includes Mont Blanc, the highest peak not only in France but in all of Western Europe as well. That's when I began to realize how close we were to France and that we soon would to be *in* it. Not more than fifteen minutes later, we docked at the French port town of Évian-les-Bains.

Several people filed off the steamer and went through what seemed like a cursory inspection of their belongings by efficient, uniformed men whom I assumed to be French customs agents. A brief look into an open satchel, an attaché case, or a picnic basket, and the debarking passengers went on their way into the picturesque spa and resort town that gently sloped up from the lake. Évian has, so my folder told me, been visited over the years by kings and princes and other luminaries and is noted for springs that for centuries have produced famous mineral waters.

The steamer took on a handful of passengers and pulled away in a northeasterly direction, as I could tell from the position of the sun. Our next stop was Lausanne, which the trusty folder told me was Switzerland's fourth-largest city and was known for its Gothic cathedral and its art and science museums.

I don't mean for this to be a travelogue, but when I am out on an assignment, Wolfe expects a full report and often details that I think of as insignificant become important to him. Fortunately, I've been blessed with something called total recall, so Wolfe gets from me all sorts of information that I would otherwise be tempted to omit.

From Lausanne, the steamer continued on to Montreux, another lake resort town and nestled against the foothills of the Alps. As at the previous stops, several people left the steamer and others boarded for the return trip to Geneva. A new crew member came aboard and I stopped him to ask about Paul Bernard, repeating my story about having met him on an earlier trip to Geneva.

"Oh yes, Paul," the bearded man responded in barely understandable English. "I have not . . . not seen him in . . . much time. I do not know why," he said with a shrug and shook his head. There was nothing more to be learned from him.

As the return trip began, I went into the steamer's largely empty café, where a steward directed me to a window table.

Perusing the limited menu, I fastened on a croque-monsieur, which was described in English as a "grilled cheese and ham sandwich on buttered bread." I ordered it, along with a glass of milk and I sat back to enjoy the view. The sandwich was tasty and unlike any ham-and-cheese sandwich I'd had before. I filed it away in my mental menu for future reference.

The trip back to Geneva seemed to go more quickly, although we still made all the same stops as before. The one difference was that larger numbers boarded than was the case on the outbound sailing, apparently drawn to Geneva for shopping, dining, or whatever other attractions that sophisticated city has to offer.

I returned to our hotel and knocked on Wolfe's door, identifying myself.

"It is unlocked," he snapped. He was in the big chair with his book and beer. "Report" was his one-word order.

It took seventeen minutes by my watch to debrief myself on the trip, during which he closed his eyes, stopping me only once. "Those customs officials in Évian that you mentioned, what was your impression of them?"

"That they seemed somewhat lax, or maybe casual is a better word, although they probably see hundreds of people pass in and out over the course of a day, what with all the steamers, tourist or otherwise, that stop in what is termed a resort town."

Wolfe raised his shoulders an inch and let them drop. "In your absence, Mr. Maillard telephoned and repeated his offer to have us dine in his establishment as his guests. I took the liberty of accepting for both of us and we have a reservation for eight tonight."

"Who am I to quarrel with your decision? I am now off to lie down and recover from a long day on the water."

The taxi ride to Émile's took ten minutes and, as we rode, I noticed Wolfe was cradling something in what appeared to be a suede bag, but I figured I would eventually find out what it was. I tipped the cabbie a decent amount and we stepped into the unpretentious ivy-covered two-story brick building, where we were greeted by none other than Émile Maillard, manning his post at the podium.

"I am so glad you were able to come on short notice," he said warmly. "I have a table ready and Philippe will be your waiter. If you have no objection, I will join you later."

"We have no objection whatever, rather the contrary," Wolfe said as Maillard led us to a table in one corner of a chandeliered dining room that was about two-thirds occupied. Philippe handed us menus as a busboy filled water glasses. "Would you like anything to drink before you order?" the waiter asked.

"Nothing for me," Wolfe said, and I concurred. After several minutes of studying what he calls the *carte*, Wolfe ordered the coq au vin while I chose the pan-fried salmon and we each ordered French onion soup for starters. Before the soup course arrived, Philippe brought a chilled wine bottle to the table.

"When Monsieur Maillard learned what you had ordered, he suggested this Sancerre from the Loire Valley." He held the bottle for Wolfe, who nodded his approval. Philippe briskly uncorked it, pouring a little into Wolfe's glass. He sniffed it, took a sip, and said, "Most satisfactory." The waiter then filled our glasses and set the bottle in a tableside wine holder filled with ice.

I felt the meal was superb and although Wolfe did not comment he did hold forth on what made the wines of France's Loire Valley so much in demand. As we were finishing our entrées,

Maillard came to our table. "Please join us, sir," Wolfe told him. "I trust your role as maître d' has concluded for the night."

"It has," our host replied with a smile as Philippe materialized with a chair for his boss. "Also, I made a command decision to select a dessert for us. It is hazelnut and crème fraîche meringues with lemon and Parmesan. I watched in the kitchen this afternoon while our pastry chef created it and I have been coveting it ever since."

Within seconds, Philippe materialized yet again, this time with a tray holding the meringues. The busboy was right behind him with the coffeepot and we dug in as Wolfe pronounced the dish "inspired."

After the dessert became history and we sipped our coffee, Wolfe bent down and pulled out the leather-covered package he had brought with him. "Mr. Maillard," he said, "it would have been churlish of us to insist upon paying for this superb meal that you so graciously offered, along with your superb choice of a wine, so in lieu of a form of repayment, Mr. Goodwin and I present this token of our thanks." With that, he pulled a bottle of Remisier brandy from the pouch he had been carrying and placed it on the table.

Maillard almost sputtered as he gaped at the label. "But . . . but this is incredible. Very little of this ambrosia exists in the world, at least as far as I know."

"You are correct, sir, and most of the bottles extant reside in my home in New York City."

"This is truly wonderful, Mr. Wolfe. It is difficult to know how to thank you both."

"You already have thanked us richly by opening up your table to us."

"I gladly accept this," Maillard said, caressing the bottle. "But that acceptance comes with a proviso."

"Tell us, sir."

"You must not return to America before you come here once again. I absolutely insist upon it."

"Very well," Wolfe said, his face creasing into a rare smile. "I believe I speak for Mr. Goodwin in saying it would be a rare pleasure to return."

"You do not have to speak for Mr. Goodwin. I am capable of doing that myself," I told Maillard with my own grin.

"Before we leave here tonight," Wolfe said, "I have yet another request and I admit it may not be something within your power."

"I am prepared with an answer," Maillard replied.

"I would very much like for Archie to get access to Paul Bernard's residence. Is this possible?"

"Would that all requests were so easy," Maillard said with a nod. "After Paul and his wife got divorced two years ago, she kept their residence as part of the agreement and I was able to get him chambers in an apartment block I own. It is a small matter for us to get the key from the block's manager, Marcel Dubois. I can go with Mr. Goodwin at any time that is convenient and I do not need to give Marcel any reason for us to seek entry to the flat."

"Satisfactory," Wolfe said.

"And I am ready to go as early as tomorrow," I put in, "if that is convenient for you."

"Tomorrow it is then," Maillard said, and we agreed on ten in the morning at the address he gave me.

CHAPTER 10

"That was a great stunt you pulled tonight," I told Wolfe as we rode back to the hotel in a cab. "But how in the world did you happen to bring the Remisier across the pond in the first place?"

"This was *not* a stunt," Wolfe insisted with a sniff. "It seemed that at some point in our voyage, it might well be beneficial to have a gift in hand. And after Mr. Maillard's generous offer to host us at his restaurant, I found the ideal individual to be the recipient of that gift."

"And in the process, you were able to get us another invitation to that gentleman's award-winning eatery."

"Such was not my intent," Wolfe said coldly.

"Okay, have it your way then. But I for one am looking forward to another visit to 'Émile's' restaurant. And I suspect that you are as well."

Wolfe remained silent for the rest of the ride.

* * *

In the morning, I stopped by Wolfe's room for instructions regarding the visit to Paul Bernard's residence.

"You hardly need instructions from me on how to search a room or a suite or an office. But I will remind you that much if not all of what you find will surely be written in French, so you may want to bring anything you find curious to me for translation. We will of course return any materials to Mr. Bernard's dwelling."

Thus instructed, I again ate in the hotel coffee shop, leaving Wolfe to consume breakfast in the silence of his room. After finishing, I took a cab to the address Maillard had given me, a fifteen-minute ride. The building, like so many other residences in Geneva, was five floors and in a formal, brick-and-stone style that I had learned from Saul Panzer was called beaux-arts. Émile Maillard stood at the front entrance, waiting for me.

"I already have telephoned Mr. Dubois," he said, "and he told me I could pick up the key to Paul's apartment at the hall man's desk in the lobby."

"And, as you suggested last night, he didn't question you?"

"No, being a loyal and efficient employee, he knows that as the building's owner, I must have a good reason for everything I do," Maillard said as we got the key and went up in the lift to the second floor, which in Europe means the third level. We went along a carpeted hall to a door marked 227.

"Paul has three rooms plus a small kitchen," Maillard said as we walked into a well-decorated living room, which looked out upon the tree-lined boulevard. "I will leave you here, Archie, to do whatever investigating you are planning, while I visit with Mr. Dubois and find out what may need attention in this money-devouring operation of mine."

After a preliminary run-through of the apartment, nothing indicated that Bernard had left suddenly. The drawers and wardrobe in his bedroom were neat and orderly and the bed was made. He had the same methodic qualities as his cousin Fritz. Perhaps it was something in the Swiss genetic makeup. A check of his nightstand found only a box of tissues, a pair of reading glasses, and an inhaler.

The kitchen was equally neat, with an empty cereal bowl and a spoon the only blemishes in an otherwise pristine sink. The living room consisted of a sofa, three chairs, two table lamps, and the small television set on a table that was becoming popular on both sides of the Atlantic.

Bernard's small, windowless office contained a desk, chair, lamp, and a three-shelf bookcase, which I focused on. As Wolfe had surmised, all of the titles were written in French, including several novels, what appeared to be a biography of John Calvin, and two volumes that I roughly translated as *A History of Lac Leman Steamers* and *Centuries of Swiss Watchmaking*, the latter of which appeared to be new or at least unused. These two books would go to Wolfe for his perusal. I opened every book and shook them out, but no mysterious pieces of paper fell out of any of them.

In the living room, I turned the cushions on the sofa and all the chairs, which showed that nothing had been sewn in the linings, sometimes a popular place to hide documents or valuables. In a similar move in the bedroom, I turned the mattress and checked the box spring, turning up nothing.

I did not feel particularly good about the session, realizing I was returning to Wolfe with nothing to show for my time.

He did not agree. "At least, we have learned that Mr. Bernard probably had not been forcibly removed from his home," he said as he drank beer and sat in what was becoming his favorite away-from-home chair. "And I would like to spend time with these books you brought back."

"I can't see where they would be of any help."

"Perhaps not, but do not be disheartened, Archie. I have something else in mind for you."

"And what might that be?"

"Get my small bag from the closet. You will find it to now be empty."

I did as was ordered and handed it to him.

"No, it's for you today," Wolfe said. "For your pistol. I assume you have brought one."

"I have, but what is this all about?"

"Put your gun in the bag and then lay a few pieces of your clothing over it to justify the bag's weight in case it gets hefted."

"Hefted? By whom?"

"A customs' agent. You are to board one of the steamers this morning and ride it as far as Évian-les-Bains."

"Then what?"

"You disembark, of course."

"And pass through customs?"

"That is the point of the exercise. It may be helpful to learn how thorough these French functionaries are."

"And I am to be the guinea pig who well help in this learning process of yours?"

"You put it well."

"And just what happens if I am stopped? What's my excuse for toting a roscoe? You may have to bail me out of the local hoosegow, that is, if they even allow bail."

"We will meet that contingency if and when it arises."

"Well, that is just great! I can see the headline now: 'American private detective jailed for carrying a firearm into peaceful resort city! His motive is being questioned by the gendarmes.'

Readers will love it. This could become an international incident."

"Your dramatics are entertaining, if overwrought."

"So, put me down as overwrought. This is just plain crazy."

"You asked earlier if I have a plan for today. This is it."

"All right, dammit. But you very well may have to leave the comfort of this room, your books, and your beer, and take a trip by whatever means to the grand old spa town of Évian to try getting me out of the lockup. The French don't figure to take kindly to foreigners bring weapons into their country."

"Dramatics has never been your strong suit, Archie."

"Yeah, well, that may be, but you're going to answer for what happens. I'm off for whatever fate awaits me."

Back at the now-familiar pier, I booked a round-trip ticket to Évian, hoping I would be able to use the second part of the ticket. The trip was uneventful, unless you count my asking a crew member if he knew "my friend," Paul Bernard, and his responding that he hadn't seen him lately and was not sure why.

We docked at Évian, with at least twenty of us leaving the steamer, a few carrying picnic baskets and fishing rods. As I had seen before, the customs' men gave quick glances at all the gear being toted ashore. I received a "*bonjour*" from one of them and returned the greeting in kind, hoping my pronunciation was acceptable.

The young man, who looked to be in his twenties, pointed to my bag, which I unzipped. He looked inside, nodded, and gestured me to move on and make way for others in the line. I left the pier, passing the red, white, and blue French flag on its pole flapping in the breeze, and took a long, deep breath.

When I reboarded to return to Geneva, I would pass through customs once again and I hoped for the same result. I had not seen any customs' officials when my earlier sailing ended in Geneva, so apparently Swiss officials were not concerned about passengers who may have boarded a steamer for their neighboring country.

If nothing else, I had pleasant time wandering along the winding streets of this old lake city, seeing all manner of clothing on the pedestrians and hearing several languages—even English on occasion. I assumed many had come for the curative waters that had made the place so famous two centuries ago, while others seemed to be headed for swimming, fishing, or the casino, doomed to enrich its coffers.

But it was time to test the French customs operation once again. I approached the dock in a line of some fifteen Geneva-bound passengers and came face-to-face with the same young man who had given my bag that very light once-over earlier. He recognized me, smiled, and passed me through without a question.

"Well, you were correct," I told Wolfe when I was back in his room, where he was of course drinking beer. "The border guards are far from thorough in checking out baggage."

"The outcome was to be expected," he said, "given your earlier description as to how lax the French authorities appear to be. But in your absence, there has been a troubling development."

"Go on," I said, sitting.

"I received a telephone call from Mr. Maillard minutes ago. He has received a call from the Geneva police saying that Paul Bernard has been seen."

"I'll be damned. Tell me more."

"We both will let Mr. Maillard be the one to tell us more. He is en route and should arrive in the next few minutes."

When Émile entered our room, he was not the ebullient host he had been in his restaurant. He appeared drawn and his brow was deeply furrowed.

"Please sit down," Wolfe urged. "May we get you something to drink?"

"Mr. Wolfe, I don't want to impose, but—"

"Nonsense! What would you prefer? Archie will order for you from room service and they also can bring me beer."

"Scotch, please, with water."

I telephoned the orders downstairs as Wolfe continued.

"You said very little on the telephone, Mr. Maillard. Supply Archie and me with details. Leave nothing out."

"This morning, just after nine, I received a call at home from a Geneva Canton policeman, who had been aware of my reports about Paul Bernard being missing. He said that a gendarme in France's Haute-Savoie region thought he had spotted Paul wandering and apparently dazed in a wooded area in the hills above Évian."

"How would Paul have been recognized by this gendarme?" Wolfe asked.

"I had given a recent photo of him to the police here, whom I have been told work closely with law officers in the adjoining areas of France, including Haute-Savoie, of which Évian is a component."

"Was Bernard on foot when he was spotted?" I put in.

"Yes, according to the constable who telephoned me. He said the gendarme called out to Paul—if that is truly who it was— and that he fled into the woods."

"Was any effort made to catch him?"

"I asked that question, Mr. Goodwin, and the response was that because Paul is not sought for any crime, the gendarme saw no reason to pursue him."

"Live and let live," Wolfe said as the waiter entered with the drink order. "Mr. Maillard, I am somewhat familiar with Geneva and its economy, but I would like to hear from you what the city is primarily known for."

"It is home to Europe's United Nations European operations and also the headquarters of the International Red Cross."

"Perhaps I should be clearer, sir. For what tangible goods is the city known?"

Maillard thought for a moment. "We are of course famous for our chocolate, our music boxes, our Swiss Army knives, and . . . but of course!" he said, snapping his fingers.

"However could I have omitted this? Most of all, I believe, Geneva is perhaps best known for our clocks and watches, watches that are said to be the finest in the world."

"Are most of these timepieces produced locally?" Wolfe asked.

"They are, sir. I happen to know that one of the biggest of the watchmakers has four facilities in the Geneva Canton that produce all of the components for their watches and also do the assembly of the final product. And another of the famous brands locates all three of its fabricating centers in Geneva. The world comes to us for its watches," Maillard said. "Now I suppose I am sounding like a member of the tourist board."

"There is no shame in taking pride in one's community," Wolfe said. "And it would seem that there is much of which to be proud in Geneva."

"Do you have any thoughts about how we can locate Paul?" Maillard asked, returning to the subject of his visit.

"You can be of aid, Mr. Maillard. It would be helpful if you could learn from the police the specific location in those wooded hills where Mr. Bernard was seen—assuming, of course, that it was he."

"I will do that."

"Also, can we get another copy of that photo of Mr. Bernard?" I asked Maillard, anticipating my next assignment from Wolfe.

"Of course, Mr. Goodwin. I have had several copies made and will bring one of them to you."

After Maillard left, I turned to Wolfe. "Am I correct in believing that I will soon be tromping around the hills above Évian?"

"You are correct and you should be prepared to depart soon after Mr. Maillard reports back to us."

"Was there a specific reason you wanted me to test the immigration staff at Évian?"

"Let us say I had an itch that needed to be scratched."

"I know how much it amuses you to speak in riddles, if that was a riddle, and I have amused you enough for now. We may now have a lead on Paul Bernard's whereabouts, but where does that leave us regarding Fritz?'

"I suspect if we are able to locate Mr. Bernard, we also will find Fritz."

"Why in God's name would one or both of them be hiding, if that's what they are, in some wooded foothills of the Alps?"

Wolfe drank beer and set his glass down. "Archie, you may very well be the one who discovers the answer to that question."

"Possibly, but right now I am sure of only one thing: that I'll have the company of my Marley .38 when I go up into those damned hills."

CHAPTER 11

It was just before noon the next day when Émile Maillard stopped by the hotel and Wolfe summoned me to his room. "I have got what you had requested," Maillard told us. "A photograph of Paul and a map that indicates the area where they said he had been seen. I drove over to Évian and got it from someone I know well at the police headquarters there, which is why I am coming to you only now."

"You should have told me where I could get the map," I said, "and I would have picked it up myself. I have gotten to know Évian so well that I could now find my way around with my eyes closed."

Maillard smiled politely at my lame stab at humor. "The divisional *commissaire* in Évian is a very good friend of mine—René Bouchard. He and his wife have often eaten in my restaurant. I thought nothing of going to his office and telling him the situation regarding Paul, and he gave the map and the photo."

Maillard then gave me the map and a photo of Bernard. The spot where he had supposedly been seen was marked in pen with an "X" on a footpath that looked according to the map's scale to be about three kilometers up the slope from the center of the spa town, which hugged the shoreline of Lake Geneva.

"Thank you very much for your efforts, sir," Wolfe said. "We will of course report any developments to you."

"And I thank you both," our visitor responded. "I should have told you earlier that I am every bit as concerned about Fritz as I am about Paul. This has been terrible for each of us."

After Maillard had left, I said to Wolfe, "What are your instructions before I set off into the wilds of the Évian hinterlands?"

"Find people who speak English. Ask questions, a skill you have honed over the years. Use your intelligence guided by experience. And do not leave for this venture until you have eaten lunch. Science has confirmed that a brain functions far better on a full stomach."

Obeying my employer, I consumed a croque monsieur, an apple pie slice, and a glass of milk in the hotel coffee shop while Wolfe dined in his room, presumably on a more substantial meal that was augmented no doubt by beer.

I wore jeans, a turtleneck sweater, rubber-soled shoes, and a leather jacket just thick enough that it nicely concealed the Marley .38 nestled in my shoulder holster. I felt like a commuter as I boarded a soon-to-depart Montreux-bound steamer. I had been riding these boats often enough lately that I now recognized several of the crew members. If I kept this up, soon we would be calling one another by our first names.

I hopped off the steamer at Évian's pier along with a handful of other riders, getting a nod and nothing more from a bored French customs guy I had not seen before. I wound my way through the narrow streets of the resort town's thronged business and shopping area and pulled out the police map of the region, which was well detailed.

I located the footpath that led upward toward the spot where Paul Bernard was said to have been seen. As I left Évian behind and began the climb on a brisk and sunny afternoon, I saw the snow-covered summit of Mont Blanc in stark contrast to the backdrop of a blue and cloudless sky.

I had not been exercising lately, as my legs were reminded me on the trek, and I stopped to catch my breath, wishing I had a canteen of water. As the scrub brush gave way to dense stands of pines and other types of trees, I had reached the map's "X," a nondescript clearing where the path I had been on intersected with another one at right angles.

I took the new path and almost immediately came across a neatly bearded hiker wearing a beret and using a walking stick. "*Bonjour*," he said with a smile and I returned the greeting, hoping my reply had some semblance of a French accent. I pulled Paul Bernard's photo out of my pocket and turned to him, asking if he spoke English.

He waggled one hand, palm down, a gesture I took to mean "a little" and I showed him the picture, saying, "Have you seen this man?"

He stroked his van dyke and frowned. "No, I do not believe so, monsieur. Have you lost him?" His English was all right, with a hint of the British Isles.

"I suppose I have," I replied. "He was last seen around here." He moved his shoulders up and down in what I was to learn is a "gallic shrug," then strode off briskly, carrying his walking stick but not seeming to need it. He was easily twenty-five years my senior and I hoped that if and when I reached his age I would be as mobile.

I found that many Swiss and French spoke varying degrees of English and it was sobering to realize that the sole extent of my foray into foreign tongues consisted of two years of high-school Latin—hardly a useful language.

I continued along the path to the left of the intersection, planning to later double back and explore to the right. There were occasional glades, breaking up the forest, and at one of them sat three small cabins well separated from one another. These were not the type of log cabin like the one where Abraham Lincoln was born, but were made of some sort of unfinished, light-colored wood.

I rapped on the rough-hewn door of one cabin several times, getting no answer. I tried the door: locked. I got the same result at the second one, getting no response and a locked door. At the third, a small, bent-over woman pulled open the door a few inches and peered at me. "Have you seen this man?" I asked, holding the picture of Bernard and hoping she spoke English. She apparently did not speak English and apparently did not like my looks, either. I knew how a vacuum cleaner salesman must feel after getting a door slammed in his face.

At another glade farther along the path, I encountered a dozen or so young people lolling around the remains of a campfire and listening to a banjo player. The men were bearded, the women long-haired, bareheaded, and wearing sandals. Many of them were smoking a certain type of warped little cigarette that is not sold in packages. Taken together, they appeared to be a group of "hippies," to use a term that was now becoming popular in the States.

"Hey, this looks to be a Yank, what with those togs," one of the men said in a slurred English, pointing at me. "What brings you to this forsaken little corner of the world, Americano? It can't be what your type would call sightseeing, not up here."

"No, it's not," I said, approaching them. "I am looking for a man." I pulled out Bernard's photo and held it up.

Several of them got to their feet and gathered around, peering at the picture. "Friend of yours who got lost?" one of the young women asked in an accent I guessed to be German.

"Something like that," I answered. "Have any of you seen him? He was in this area in the last few days."

I was met with blank expressions and head-shaking. The curiosity that had been piqued by my arrival on the scene quickly worn off and, one by one, the crew sat back down as the banjo player resumed strumming. I had become invisible.

I won't bore you with the rest of my trek in the foothills, as there is nothing to report. I returned to the hotel, where Wolfe—no surprise—was reading in his room with two bottles of beer and a stein as company.

After I filled him in on my afternoon of futility, he drew in a bushel of air and exhaled. "I am not surprised at your lack of success, but we invariably cling to hope. I assume Geneva has a daily newspaper."

"Probably more than one," I said. "I remember seeing a stack of papers called *Le Tribune de Genève* on the check-in counter downstairs."

"Get one," he said. Here is vintage Wolfe, barking an order without so much as a "please" thrown in. But then, I have long since gotten used to his manner. I went downstairs and returned with a copy of the tabloid newspaper, handing it to him.

He scanned the headlines, then flipped through the rest of the pages, scowling. "What are you looking for?" I asked.

"A telephone number. I wish to communicate with the publication's offices."

Typical Wolfe: Impatient and demanding. I took the paper from him and found the number on the second page. Without asking him, I called downstairs and asked the hotel operator to dial the number. When I heard the ringing, I handed the instrument to Wolfe.

For the next several minutes, I listened to the conversation, which was dominated by Wolfe speaking in French, presumably to someone at the newspaper. After ringing off, he turned to me. "You are to go to the *Tribune* offices with the photograph of Mr. Bernard. They will give you a proof of what I just dictated to their representative. Bring it back here to me."

"Yes, sir," I said, saluting, which earned me a glower. I went down to the lobby where the man behind the counter gave me the address of the paper. A cabbie drove me to a part of Geneva I had not been to, which clearly was the city's commercial center, complete with streetcars, or what the Swiss call trams, often coupled together in pairs, that navigate the city's narrow and curving streets. I got dropped off at a three-story building near the railway station that held a rooftop sign proclaiming the newspaper's name in large letters.

In the building's lobby, an arrow marked *Publicité* pointed to a room on the right, which I walked into. A fashionable young blonde woman behind a counter smiled and in excellent English asked, "You have come here from Monsieur Wolfe, no?"

"How ever did you guess?"

"When I spoke to him on the telephone, he described you very well," she said with a smile that showed dimples and perfect teeth.

I took her expression to mean that she liked what she saw, but then I was reminded of what Lily Rowan once told me: "You may like to think, Escamillo, that you are God's gift to women, but that gift could very well be overrated." That was her way of saying, "Don't be too full of yourself."

"I am here to get something from you, I believe," I said.

"Yes, this is it, Monsieur Goodwin," she said, handing me an envelope. "And you have a photograph for me?"

"I do." The switch completed, I departed, leaving her with a smile, which got returned.

When I gave Wolfe what I had got at the *Tribune*, I said, "It is good to know that Swiss newspapers, like their American counterparts, run 'Have you seen this man?' advertisements in their pages. I assume that's what is going on here. I also assume that in the copy, you have included a cash reward for anyone who comes up with verifiable information as to Bernard's whereabouts."

"Your assumptions are correct," he said. "After I have approved this copy and given said approval to the newspaper by telephone, they will then set up the advertisement with the photograph and put together a proof, which you will pick up and bring back here."

"So nice to know I am being of some humble use to you. At this rate, I'll get to know every taxi driver in Geneva on a first-name basis." Wolfe OK'd the copy, which I took back to the newspaper office. I was told by the same young woman that they would in a half hour have a completed proof of the ad, with photo, which would then run in the next day's editions. While I waited, I paid the fee for the insertion.

Because I can't read French, I was not able to sign off on the proof, so back to Wolfe I went with it. He read through the copy, nodded, and called the newspaper office, telling them (I assume) to go ahead.

Similar to the practice in American newspapers, the *Tribune* included a postal number in the advertisement where readers could respond and, we hoped, report on where and when they had seen the man in the picture. That meant, of course, more cab rides to the newspaper's offices to pick up the hoped-for responses.

My taxi trips continued the next afternoon, well past the delivery time of the early editions of the newspaper. I picked up four envelopes that had arrived by messenger at the newspaper, jumping into yet another taxi and heading back to our hotel.

Wolfe read the replies rapidly and muttered. "Pah, nothing of any substance here," he growled after translating the material he had gotten from the *Tribune* readers. "It's clear that none of these individuals had seen Mr. Bernard. They are just looking to make some easy money."

"But hasn't that been the case back home with so many of the 'Have you seen this person?' ads that you've placed in the *Gazette* and the *New York Times*? We've had a lot more strikeouts than hits."

"Yes, you are correct, of course. However, we also have had enough success over time to warrant continuing the practice, wouldn't you agree?"

"I would, especially given where we are right now, which is, let's face it, up the creek without a paddle."

Wolfe made a face, as he so often does with my figures of speech (or whatever you call them). "We will place the item in the newspaper for two more days and then reevaluate our strategy, do you agree?"

"Yep. At the moment, I don't see any decent alternative," I said.

The next morning after breakfast, I thought about how, up to now, my Swiss visit had been divided into two segments. The first was steamer rides, a batch of them, and now I have made so many trips by taxi that I've now gotten the same hackie three times—counting today.

"Nice to see you again," my driver said in what I took to be an Italian accent as we pulled away from the hotel and headed to the newspaper office. "If you need me again, I am usually right over there in front of the railroad station," he told me with a grin.

I grinned back and went into the newspaper building and to the office where answers to advertisements were kept. I was pleased to see that we had a batch of eight responses. Back in the street, I saw the taxi I had arrived in, parked as he had said at the curb in front of the station.

"Right where you said you would be," I told to the driver, whose name I learned was Guido. He told me he had lived in Geneva for a dozen years and hailed from a small town called Domodossola in the Italian Alps. "No jobs there," he said as we pulled away, bound for the hotel. "I heard that things were better in Suisse so I came and, after I found this work, I brought my lady here from Italy and we got married and now I have two sons. That is my story."

"Quite a story indeed. You speak English very well," I told him.

"It is important to know several languages. Here in this job of always meeting people, you have to speak at the very least French and English and preferably German as well. I am what you would call a 'fast learner,' is that right to say?"

"Yes, it is, and a good thing to be. You also speak Italian too, of course."

"It is helpful sometimes also." Guido said, going on to tell me about some of the important people he had driven in Geneva, including a couple of ambassadors, a gospel singer, and an Arab sheik. As I paid him and hopped out of his cab at the hotel, I wished Guido well. His response: "We may meet once again."

CHAPTER 12

When I went up to Wolfe's hotel room and knocked on the door, the response was, "Come in, Archie; it is unlocked."

I entered and found him on his feet, looking out onto Lake Geneva. "This lake is in reality part of a river, as well," he said. "The Rhone, which rises in the Alps, traverses the lake's entire length and then goes through the city of Geneva before running south through the French communities of Lyon, Avignon, and Arles and emptying into the Mediterranean."

"Always happy to get a history lesson, or in this instance, a geography lesson. I probably learned about the Rhone in high school, but that was a long time ago. Back to the present: I bring you more responses," I said, holding up the sheaf of responses.

"Yes, back to the present indeed," Wolfe replied, planting himself in the room's largest chair and beginning to read and translate. I watched as he tossed one response after another aside, muttering under his breath. Then, he sat upright and blinked. "Archie, may I read this to you? I ask that advisedly, as you know that I do not like being read to myself."

"Read away," I replied, taking a chair myself. "I also don't much like being read to, but in this case, I will make an exception."

Wolfe dipped his chin in a nod, cleared his throat, and began:

"*I do not know the name of the man in your picture, but I do know something about who he is. I live in Genève and I travel often to Évian because of shops there I like to patronize and also a favorite café, which has wonderful soufflés. I have seen this man at the helm, if that is the right term, as captain of my steamer several times on these trips. I also have seen him in his uniform on the quay before sailings, laughing with passengers and other crew members. He seemed a most commanding and personable figure, often in conversations. I never have spoken to him, however.*

"*On one visit to Évian about a fortnight ago, I happened to see him on the street, not in his uniform. He was with another man who appeared to be very angry with him. There was shouting, but they were too far away for me to hear what was being said. It seemed surprising to me that a man who seemed so friendly and so respected was also very frightened. I don't know if this aids you in any way, but I can tell you it was a most unsettling experience for me.*"

Wolfe put down the correspondence and turned to me. "Your thoughts?"

"Number one, pay the woman—assuming it is a woman. Number two, invite her in to a friendly conversation."

"The name in the missive is Celine Laurent," Wolfe said, "with an address and number in Geneva. I will telephone her."

And he did, speaking in French, of course. I was unable to

get the gist of their conversation, or rather, Wolfe's side of it, although I did hear him use the word *anglais*. After hanging up, he said, "She seemed surprised to hear from an American, but she brightened when told she would be given a financial reward. I suggested that she come here and was told she would meet only in a public part of the hotel, not in this room."

"Hey, a woman can't be too careful these days, especially where Americans men are concerned. Maybe some of the G.I.'s during or after the war left lasting impressions on the local mademoiselles and even madams. We don't know which she is. By the way, I heard you use the French word for 'English.'"

"I asked the woman if she spoke it and she answered in the affirmative. She will be here at three and I told her to meet us in the coffee shop," Wolfe said.

Wolfe and I were at a table in the coffee shop several minutes before three when a full-figured, well-dressed woman of perhaps fifty entered, looked around, and then spotted us with a nod. We both stood as she approached the table and said, "I am Madame Laurent." She held out a hand that both Wolfe and I each held briefly, Wolfe reluctantly, given his distaste for physical contact.

"Please be seated, madam," he said in English. "I am Nero Wolfe and this is my associate, Mr. Goodwin. Which language would you prefer to converse in?"

"English in fine with me," she said as she eased into a chair facing Wolfe. "I have spoken it for many years. I work for the United Nations here and it is helpful in my job to speak several languages."

"Will you have something to eat?" Wolfe asked. "And perhaps coffee?"

"Coffee would be good," she replied.

Wolfe had the waiter come over and he ordered a pot of coffee and small pastries.

"Mr. Goodwin and I were intrigued by your letter," Wolfe said, "to the extent that we will give you remuneration." He nodded in my direction and I handed an envelope to Mme. Laurent, who took it, unopened, and slipped it into her purse. "Thank you," she said to me with the hint of a smile. And to Wolfe: "I wrote all I know about the man in the photograph and I do not believe I am able to add anything more."

"Perhaps you are correct, madam, but as long as you were kind enough to come to meet with us, I would like to see if it is possible for you to expand upon your reminiscence."

"I will answer anything I am able to," she said. "First, I have a question." He nodded.

"I admit to being curious about the name of the gentleman in question and why you are interested in him."

"Those are two questions, madam. He is Paul Bernard and, as you observed, he has for many years been a captain on lake steamers. As to why Mr. Goodwin and I are interested in him, that response will have to wait."

"Understood," she said, again with a slight smile.

"Now, before we get to Mr. Bernard," Wolfe said, "you have written that you frequently pass from Switzerland into France and back again. Do you find this regular intercountry travel to be an inconvenience?"

"Not at all, Mr. Wolfe. The two nations get along very well and each makes travel between them uncomplicated."

"Which might lead one to ask if smuggling from one country to the other has ever been a problem. Have you, as a United Nations employee, at any time been aware of illegal commerce across the border?"

"Nothing I have ever heard of," she answered, turning her palms up.

"Back to Mr. Bernard. You seem to have been impressed by his bearing."

"The few times I have observed him interacting with others, he has seemed most personable and engaging, which is why I was shocked at the animosity between the two men, particularly on the part of the other man."

"Can you describe that man?"

"Not very well, I am afraid, as I saw him for such a short time. I do remember that he was quite a bit taller than Mr. . . . Bernard, is it? And quite thin."

Wolfe nodded and the woman continued. "His hair was dark, almost black, and he had many tattoos on both of his arms: hearts, crosses, a lightning bolt. Why I remember that I am not sure, but it stood out to me in the moment. Also . . ." she paused, wrinkling a brow as if in thought . . . "he had an earring in one ear, the right one, I believe."

"Were you close enough to hear him talk?" I put in, adding, "and if so, did he have a particular accent?"

Another wrinkled brow. "What I mainly heard was his threatening tone and if pressed I would say it was in French, although from where I stood, I would not have been able to identify a regional dialect in the few words I picked up."

"What were those words?" Wolfe asked.

"Oh my . . . you are certainly testing me. I do know there were two or three curse words, words that I would never use. And he told Mr. Bernard something like "you will regret . . ." and that is all I picked up."

"What was the last you saw of the men?"

"The went away separately, in different directions, with the aggressive one shaking a fist and saying something I couldn't hear.

Mr. Bernard was almost running. That was the last I saw of either of them, although I've been back to Évian at least twice since then."

"And no sign of Mr. Bernard, of course?" I asked.

"No, not at all."

"Thank you for your letter and for taking the time to see us, madam," Wolfe said.

"And thank you for this, sir?" she answered, pointing at the envelope with the money she had yet to see as she prepared to get up. "I may be speaking out of turn here, but I have to ask: Are you an agent of some government, perhaps the United States? You sound like you are an American."

"I am not an agent for any organization, madam, but merely a private citizen who finds the disappearance of Paul Bernard to be most troubling, for reasons I am not prepared to discuss. And as you correctly ascertained, I am an American, as is my colleague."

"You are indeed a man of mystery, Mr. Wolfe, and perhaps at some time in the future, I will understand what all this has been about."

"It is possible you will, Madame Laurent," he said as she rose and held out a hand, which he shook as he had no alternative.

After she had gone, Wolfe and I both stood up. "I hope that her not recognizing your name did not bruise you too much," I said. "But after all, Geneva probably doesn't get all that much news from the States."

For the second time since we had undertaken this project, Wolfe said "Shut up, Archie," and as before, I replied "Yes, sir."

CHAPTER 13

The next morning after I had gone down to the coffee shop to take sustenance, I went to Wolfe's room, where he was just polishing off breakfast.

"Hope it was filling," I told him. "I assume you would like me to go to the newspaper office and collect any responses we've gotten."

"Your assumption is correct."

"If we haven't gotten anything more by this time, we may be beating a dead horse."

"I prefer to think we have a live horse, Archie, and that it may very well be a longshot. I am told they sometimes win."

"Hey, I'm fine with the assignment. I've even gotten to know the name of the local railway depot, almost next door to the newspaper. For the record, it's Cornavin Station."

"It is good to hear you are aware of your surroundings," Wolfe remarked, turning to his book. That was my cue to leave.

I did not know my cabbie on this trip and he wasn't the chatty type, which was fine with me. I was getting somewhat discouraged, even with Mrs. Laurent's moderately interesting report, and I found myself in a testy mood.

At the newspaper, I was given an envelope containing a half dozen more responses, which if nothing else showed that Genevans, if that is what they are called, have an interest in money. When I got back to the hotel and to Wolfe's room, I found him reading the book from Paul Bernard's apartment about Swiss watchmaking.

"Most interesting," he remarked, then turned to me wearing a questioning expression.

"Here they are, for what it's worth," I said, handing over the latest batch of attempts by readers of the *Tribune* get money out of us. As Wolfe waded through the responses, I walked down the hall to my room to brush my teeth and run a comb through my hair.

When I returned, he said, "Can you tolerate my reading to you again?"

"I can tolerate anything, if it helps to get us off dead center."

He started, "*Of course I immediately recognized Paul when I saw the advertisement and I suppose many other readers did as well, given how well known he is in certain circles, so my response may not be all that surprising. But in case no one else has come forward to identity him and tell at least part of his story, perhaps what I have to tell you may be of some use. Paul Bernard for years has been a lake steamer captain, one of the best and best-liked people in the entire fleet. A more capable and dependable officer I have yet to encounter.*

"*Recently, however, Paul has been haunted by the knowledge of dark activities over which he has no control. This knowledge has become a liability to him and it almost certainly is the reason he has disappeared. Where he is, I do not know, but I can only hope that he is safe.*

"I do not want my name known publicly, but I have attached a telephone number, if you wish to reach me."

"What is your reaction?" Wolfe asked when he had finished.

"One of puzzlement, but then, I know you will be quick to respond that I am easily puzzled. As with the woman we talked to, I vote that we meet with this nameless gentleman."

"It is unanimous. Dial his number," Wolfe said as he handed me the letter.

Wolfe knows perfectly well how to use a telephone, but he is comfortable giving orders, particularly to me. The hotel operator dialed for me and after three rings, a male voice answered, *"Oui?"*

I handed the receiver over. "Sir, I have read your letter and I am most interested in meeting you." Wolfe spoke in French, but I am pretty sure that is the essence of what he said.

The man at the other end must have given a positive response, because after both men had exchanged more words, Wolfe hung up and said, "The gentleman will be at the hotel in a half hour and we will talk with him in an alcove off the lobby, as I suggested."

"His name?"

"He chose not to give it and I did not press the issue. We may eventually learn his identity, but for now, the important thing is to find out what, if anything, he knows about the whereabouts of Bernard and ultimately of Fritz as well. I assume you agree?"

"Absolutely. And like you, I am very curious about what 'Mister X' has to say to us."

We had settled at a table in quiet nook tucked into a corner of the lobby when a bearded man of perhaps fifty peered into the darkness of our recess and squinted.

"Do you speak English, sir?" Wolfe asked and when he received a nod he continued. "I am the man to whom you spoke on the telephone. Please join us."

"I recognize the voice," our visitor said in a tone laced with French as he took the third chair at the table. If he was surprised at Wolfe's size, he did not show it.

"This man is my associate and we both found your letter to be most interesting, sir."

"May I assume that you are the individual who placed the notice and picture in the *Tribune*?"

"You may. How do you happen to know Paul Bernard?"

"We have been coworkers for many years," came the reply and I realized seeing him close up that the man was older than I had originally thought, his face deeply lined and with a tan that had settled in for life.

"It is clear from your message that you are concerned about Mr. Bernard."

"I am and I have a question: Have you received other letters from those who have worked with or for Paul?"

"We have not," Wolfe said, having decided that we were to be open with those responding.

"Although I'm sure many who work on the steamers will have recognized Paul's photograph in what is Geneva's most-read newspaper, I am not surprised at the lack of response."

"Why is that?" I asked.

"Fear, fear for their personal safety."

"Please continue," Wolfe prodded.

"I do not know all of what is happening, but it seems that

people I have never before seen are riding the steamers, at least as far as Évian."

"Can you describe them?"

Our mystery man pressed his palms against his eyes. "Men who . . . who do not seem like our typical passengers."

"Continue."

"They are not what one might term . . . *genteel* and most of those normally riding the steamers are civilized and amiable folk—tourists riding the lake, fishermen, swimmers, and sailors going to Évian, shoppers and diners enjoying what many of the lake cities like Lausanne and Montreux have to offer, and sightseers visiting the Castle of Chillon."

"How long have these ignoble individuals been prevalent as riders on the steamers?" Wolfe posed.

"I find that difficult to say, because their presence had been a gradual thing at first, one or maybe two of them on board."

"How were they dressed?"

"In no particular manner. I suspect they were trying not to call attention to themselves."

"No doubt. What, if anything, were they carrying?" I asked.

"In some instances, at least one of them had a leather bag of sorts with a shoulder strap, not large at all."

Wolfe shut his eyes and for a moment I thought he might be starting to push his lips out and in, out and in, a sign that he is about to make a pronouncement. But it was not to be and he merely shook his head once and opened his eyes.

He looked at our guest and asked, "Where do these men board and leave the steamer?"

"They invariably get on here in Geneva and almost without exception debark at Évian."

"Do you have a theory on why that is the case?"

"I must never be connected with this conversation," was the

whispered reply, "but I believe, as do many other crew members who are afraid to speak, that a smuggling ring has insinuated itself into the steamer line."

"What contraband is being smuggled?" Wolfe asked.

"I do not know that but, whatever it is, those behind the ring are serious and dangerous and I believe they are responsible for the disappearance of Paul Bernard."

"Is it your sense that Mr. Bernard had learned about what was going on?" I asked.

"Yes. I have often served as first mate on Paul's steamer and one time, when we were together on the bridge, he gestured down to a passenger who was leaving us at Évian and said, 'That man bears watching' or something like that. When I asked what he meant, Paul turned away and said nothing, as if he already had said too much."

Wolfe turned to me and dipped his chin, a signal to pay our still-unnamed visitor. "You have given us much to think about," he said as I handed the man an envelope containing a batch of francs.

"I did not come here solely seeking money, but I can always use it, even though I have only myself to support. I have never married and have no family. Our small country with its neutrality got spared the horrors of the war, but that does not mean that all is well. Thank you," he said, rising and headed for the exit.

"Your thoughts?" I asked Wolfe, as I so often do.

"Our nameless man clearly is frightened, Archie. He may very well be correct about smugglers using his company's vessels and that he is the only one from the steamer line to respond to our published appeal suggests he is not alone in his unease."

CHAPTER 14

In our few days in Geneva, Wolfe, always an avid newspaper reader, had acquired the habit of having the room service waiter bring up the day's issue of *Le Times* with his breakfast. It was to bring sobering news this day.

When I went to Wolfe's room after finishing my own breakfast downstairs, he held the paper out to me, with is first section folded back to page three. Wolfe, who translated the headline as man shot on street, also translated the short item, which read:

Last night, a man identified as Lucien Leclerc, 58, of Geneva, was found dead on the Rue du Rhône pavement from a bullet wound, according to police. A nearby resident reported hearing a gunshot. The police said that robbery apparently was not the motive for the killing, as the dead man's wallet and watch were untouched and he was carrying 40 Swiss francs in an envelope in his pocket. "It is extremely rare to have shootings in the City Center," a police spokesman said.

M. Leclerc worked as a crew member on lake steamers out of Geneva. He leaves no survivors, according to the ship company.

"He might not be our man," I told Wolfe, not buying my comment for a second.

"Perhaps not, but I have never been a believer in coincidences and what we have here are coincidences. For one, you gave forty francs to the man who we now believe to be Lucien Leclerc. At the moment, we need not concern ourselves with the dead man."

"Agreed. I sense an assignment coming. And I think I know what it is."

"Let us see if we are of one mind, Archie. It is more important than ever that you ride the lake boats—but again, only as far as Évian. It is of little matter that you do not speak French. Your eyes will be your greatest asset, although they should be supplemented by a firearm."

"Oh, they will be," I told him.

So, it was back to the dock to purchase a ticket with a return and wait for the next steamer, due to leave in fifteen minutes. I boarded, wearing sunglasses, a windbreaker, and a flat cap. Maybe I looked like an American, although there were at least a couple of other similarly garbed men on this run and I heard one of them speaking in French.

I studied all of the passengers on both of the decks from behind my shades. Most of them looked to be typical vacationers or shoppers, although one man sitting near the stern of the upper deck stood out. While almost everyone else was admiring the natural beauty of the surroundings or chatting among themselves, this guy seemed tense and jittery, his eyes darting in all directions, but at nothing or no one in particular. And he toted a leather shoulder bag, much like our nameless source said he had seen being carried on the steamers.

When the boat docked at Évian, the man with his leather bag and I were among the score of riders who disembarked. Passing into France was its usual snap, with the smartly uniformed customs officer merely nodding and smiling or saluting as the passengers filed past him.

I stayed well behind my man as he left the dock and stepped onto the street that paralleled the shoreline, which was bustling with pedestrians in resort wear and couples, some with children, out for day in the colorful surroundings of the spa, the mineral waters, the casino, and the many other attractions offered by this resort town. He seemed out of place, as perhaps I did as well, but I did my best to blend in, thankful for the crowds that gave me cover. I have always prided myself on my ability to hold a tail, maybe not as good as Saul Panzer, but still damned effective, if I do say so myself.

Periodically, my target would stop suddenly and look around, as though suspecting he might be followed. When that happened, I would be looking into a shop window at beachwear or perfume bottles or postcards or racks of sunglasses.

He continued along the avenue for about three blocks and then handed the bag to another man in a move so slick I almost missed it. The one I am now calling Courier No. 1 did a snappy about-face and passed me going in the direction from which we had come, surely unaware he had been followed. I quickly picked up my pace and had Courier No. 2 in view as he took confident strides.

As I followed my current target at a distance, I wondered if he also would do a handoff, bringing a third party into play in a bucket-brigade type of exercise. As it turned out, he did a handoff, but of a different sort. He went up beside a small truck, similar to the type seen delivering packages on Manhattan streets, and handed his bag to the driver, whose arm came out and snatched it. Cleanly done and the truck pulled away.

I committed the vehicle's French license number to memory and I watched as Courier No. 2 walked off in the direction of the shoreline. Okay, so something was going on here, but what, exactly? I felt I had accomplished something, although I would need others to tell me what it was.

The steamer ride back to Geneva was uneventful and when I got to the hotel, Wolfe was devouring a lunch consisting of sweetbreads in bechamel sauce, a favorite of his at home. Because he has a hard-and-fast rule to not discuss business during meals, I sat on the sofa and thumbed through a picture book full of color photos of the city and the lake. When he was finished with the meal, I asked, "Were the sweetbreads as good as Fritz's?"

"No, but then, I didn't expect them to be. Report."

As always, I was detailed in describing the trip to Évian and back. Wolfe took in air and exhaled, saying, "Call Mr. Maillard. Given your memory, I assume you know the number."

I did, giving the hotel operator the number, who did the work. When Maillard answered, I handed over the receiver. "This is Nero Wolfe, sir. Would it be an imposition to ask if you could see us at the hotel at your convenience?"

"Not at all. I can be there in fifteen minutes," he said. Twelve minutes later, there was a knock on the door to Wolfe's room.

"Thank you for your promptness, sir. Archie, will you ring to have coffee brought up for us?"

Maillard parked in one of the chairs and gave Wolfe a questioning look.

"Archie has just returned from a trip to Évian and back that proved to be most enlightening. I would like you to hear his report. He will be most thorough."

And thorough I was, except for a break when the room service waiter came up with coffee. Maillard listened, nodding occasionally. When I finished, he said, "Mr. Wolfe, I know of course from Fritz of your reputation as a private detective, so I hesitate to comment on Mr. Goodwin's report."

"Come, come, sir, we are in need of your perspective. I do not patronize you by saying you can be valuable to us in areas where Archie and I have voids in our knowledge."

Maillard pondered for a moment and then said, "All right, based on what Mr. Goodwin has reported, it would seem that some sort of smuggling is going on, although it would have to involve small items, such as jewels, given the size of the packages you say are used in transporting the contraband materials."

"Have there been instances where jewels were illegally transported from Geneva to France?" Wolfe asked.

"Not to my knowledge, although if there were such instances, I would have no reason to know about them, unless they were reported in the newspapers."

"Let me suggest something other than jewels is involved."

"But what would—of course, of course, I should have thought of that!" Maillard said, slapping his hands together. "Watches!"

"Maybe," Wolfe responded, "or perhaps *parts* of watches." In response, Maillard wore a puzzled expression.

"I have been reading a book on the history of Swiss watchmaking that Archie and I found in Paul Bernard's apartment," Wolfe said. "I had known before about the high quality of watches made in this country and specifically in the Geneva area, but I now have learned a great deal more about their manufacture and am particularly impressed by the intricate detail and craftsmanship that must go into in the movements of these timepieces."

"Are you suggesting that it is the innards of watches that are being smuggled?" Maillard asked, eyebrows raised.

"I am suggesting that possibility, sir. Those complex inner workings are so small that they could be easily transported in large numbers. And from what I have read and already knew, they are extremely valuable.

"And to return to my earlier subject, we are in need of your assistance and your familiarity with the community. Archie is hamstrung by his inability to speak French and I, as you can see, am limited in my mobility."

"I certainly am willing to do whatever you suggest," Maillard said. "As I mentioned previously, I am not constrained by responsibilities. The restaurant runs very well without me— perhaps too well," he added with a sheepish grin.

"I will suggest ways in which you can be of aid to us," Wolfe said. "You have said that you are a good friend of Mr. Bouchard, the police *commissaire* in the French region that encompasses Évian. If he is not already, he may be aware of the probability that some form of smuggling is taking place in or around a large and important city in his area of responsibility. Giving him the license plate number of the vehicle Archie observed would be helpful to him."

"I agree and I will certainly try to reach him today."

"Does your network of friends in the community include executives in the watchmaking world?"

"Yes, it does. As a matter of fact, I am happy to say that among the regular patrons of the restaurant are many of the top officials at three of our leading watch companies," Maillard said. "I have known each of them for many years and you could term us good friends. I'm comfortable talking to them."

"I would like to know if any of their companies, or anyone else among the city's watchmakers, has experienced problems with the quality of the movements that are being produced," Wolfe said. "Your inquiries probably should be discreet, but then, I have no business giving such advice, because only you know the closeness of your relationship with these individuals."

"I can be the model of discretion, Mr. Wolfe," Maillard said with a grin.

"I have no doubt of it, sir, no doubt whatever."

After Maillard had left, Wolfe turned to me. "I read in this morning newspaper that a visitation has been scheduled for later this afternoon for Lucien Leclerc. I have written down the name and address of the mortuary."

"And you want me to go there and, assuming there is an open casket, confirm that the individual in said casket is the same individual we talked to."

"Your summary of the situation is accurate."

A fifteen-minute taxi ride took me to a one-story stone building on a tree-lined avenue that paralleled the Rhone River. I walked in, was greeted with a somber nod by a man in a dark suit who seemed to take a proprietary interest in the proceedings. I entered a parlor where four or five individuals, all men, stood talking. I recognized one of them as a crew member on one of the lake steamers I had ridden.

They threw me curious glances, then continued with their subdued conversation as I went over to the casket. It was no surprise that the waxy figure lying amid the silk backdrop was indeed the man Wolfe and I had met.

After what I considered to be a decent interval, I backed away from the casket and walked out of the mortuary. I again drew glances from the small gathering huddled together, all of them likely coworkers of the dead man on the lake steamers, as Bouchard had told us he had no family. These men likely were, in effect, the only family he had.

CHAPTER 15

Back at the hotel, I said to Wolfe, "If we really are dealing with a smuggling ring, which now seems likely, these people are playing for keeps, given how Lucien Leclerc ended up. Apparently, they knew he was onto them and they may have followed him to our hotel. So, they may be keeping an eye on us as well."

"That thought has occurred to me, as well," he said. "Now we wait to hear from Mr. Maillard, unless you have another plan."

"I suppose I could ride a steamer to Évian again, to see if I can learn any more of what appears to be happening."

"No, let us bide our time, Archie." As Wolfe has said before, I tend to lack patience and I was damned impatient at the moment. I needed to be doing something, but what?

Fortunately, fate stepped in a few minutes later in the form of a telephone call from Émile Maillard. After I had picked up the receiver and said hello to the restaurateur, I passed it over to Wolfe.

"Yes, sir," he said, "we are available and are eager for your information. No, I thank you for the kind offer, but this time, we would like to host you at the restaurant right here in the hotel, if that does not insult you. All right, seven o'clock then."

After signing off, Wolfe turned to me. "Mr. Maillard has been busy and appears to have much to report."

"I guess that's good news. And we're going to be dining downstairs?"

"Yes, it is our turn to play host."

At seven, Wolfe and I were already seated at a table in Chez Marc when Maillard arrived. "Do you feel you are dining in enemy territory?" I asked after he had been seated.

That drew a laugh. "Not really," he said. "We have long been friendly competitors and we both carry the same Michelin rating, making us surely the two best restaurants in the city. I've known Claude, who is in charge here, for years. Once word of my presence gets back to the kitchen, he will make an appearance, I guarantee it."

True to the prediction, a short, salt-and-pepper haired man with a mustache came to our table even before we had a chance to order drinks. "Ah, Émile," he said in accented English with a bow, "have you come to see how things are done on the lakeside of our fine city?"

"I am just checking up on you, Claude, to ensure that you are continuing to maintain high standards."

Claude reacted with a pseudo-theatrical sniff. "Perhaps it is time for me to make a visit to your own establishment and do some investigating of my own."

"You are welcome at any time, *mon ami.* I will tell the staff to be alert to your arrival and you shall be treated as a visiting royal."

"I will arrive unannounced, as a test. Now," our host went on, "I can highly recommend the *Coquilles Saint-Jacques*, with its scallops having been shipped in from the Atlantic coast of France this very day." Maillard and I chose the scallops, while Wolfe went with the *gigot d'agneau Pascal*, a dressed-up name for roast leg of lamb.

After Claude departed and wine had been served, Wolfe turned to Maillard, eyebrows raised in an unspoken question.

"On to business, at least until the entrée arrives," the Swiss said, signaling a change in the mood at the table. "I have been able to reach two of the men who are on the boards of the finest watchmakers in this country and both of them told me that a competitor of theirs, who also is the producer of a superb product, has been rejecting movements sent to them by an outside supplier. I should mention I have learned that several of our watch companies do not make their own movements, but sign contracts with organizations that have skilled artisans who design them."

"Has a reason been given for the rejection of these movements?" Wolfe asked.

"The men I spoke to said the company in question felt the intricate mechanisms being offered to them were not up to their standards."

"What happens to the rejected movements?" I asked.

"They usually are sent back to the maker," Maillard said. "And as often is the case, the watch company then selects a new supplier."

"Is this rejection of a supplier a common occurrence?"

"It is uncommon but not unprecedented, Mr. Wolfe. These watchmakers are and should be very demanding, which is why some of them make their own movements.

"I am told that other, smaller operations may not have the financial wherewithal to afford skilled movement creators on their payrolls," Maillard added. "As you can tell, I am myself learning only now about what goes on within the world of watchmaking. It is an education for me."

"I, too have been learning about the intricacies of this nonpareil world," Wolfe said, "with much of my information gathered from the book we took from Mr. Bernard's home. Did your sources tell you what happens to watch movements that have been rejected?"

"I regret to say I did not pose that question. I'm afraid I would not have made a good detective. I can go back to the men I talked to and ask."

"That is not necessary right now," Wolfe said. "It's hard to imagine these minuscule workings being destroyed, given the painstaking workmanship that has led to their creation. Who at a watchmaking company decides on the choice of the inner workings of their finely tuned chronometers?"

"I did pose that question," Maillard said, clearly pleased that he had thought to ask. "I was told that at the best of the makers, decisions on the innards go all the way to the top. At the smaller operations, someone lower down the line makes the decisions."

"Did your sources suggest that there may have been any type of questionable dealings involving the selection or purchase of movements?"

"One of them did tell me that there had been rumors of money changing hands in dealings between suppliers and watchmakers, but he said he had no concrete information or confirmations of . . . irregular behavior."

"No doubt in this closed and secretive world, with information being hard to come by," Wolfe observed with a sour expression. "Has your friend with the French police had any success regarding that truck Mr. Goodwin saw in Évian?"

"Ah, I was about to bring the subject around to my friend René Bouchard," Maillard said, looking uneasy. "He would very much like to meet with you and Mr. Goodwin. I am afraid I have committed a *faux pas*."

"How so, sir?" Wolfe asked.

"I told him your name."

"Indeed. I did not realize I was in Switzerland incognito."

"I thought perhaps I had misspoken by using your name," Maillard said, relieved. "René was most impressed and he wants to meet you. He has heard about you and your reputation in America."

Nobody knows Wolfe better than I do and, although he tries with success to hide it, I know how much he likes to be acknowledged, whether it be with compliments or mentions and photographs in newspapers.

"I would be willing to meet Mr. Bouchard," Wolfe told Maillard.

"Excellent! He has invited you and Mr. Goodwin to visit him at his office in Évian-les-Bains. I can drive you both there."

That jolted Wolfe, who expects people to come to him, not the reverse. But he was in a pickle here and was faced with having to ride in a car driven by someone other than me. I was curious to see how he would handle this dilemma.

"Very well," he said, veiling any discomfort he felt. "When would he like to meet with us?"

"He suggested tomorrow morning, at a time of your convenience."

Wolfe said after a pause, "Archie and I can be there at nine o'clock." That's just like him, making appointments for me without bothering to ask. Okay, so maybe my calendar wasn't full, but it would have been nice to be consulted.

* * *

The next morning, Émile Maillard pulled up in front of our hotel in his Mercedes sedan a few minutes before nine. Wolfe stood on the sidewalk in full traveling garb of fur-collared coat, scarf, pirate hat and, of course, his walking stick. I climbed into the front seat with Maillard while Wolfe got the back seat to himself. I was pleased to see that the car was outfitted with a hand strap similar to the one my boss gripped so tightly while riding in our Heron with either me or Saul Panzer behind the wheel.

If Wolfe was bothered by Maillard's driving, which seemed fine to me, he didn't show it. We left Geneva and followed the lake's shoreline until we came to the French border and the customs barrier. As with passengers on the steamers who entered France, the procedure was cursory, with a uniformed sentry peering into the car, nodding and waving us through with a snappy salute.

"It's pretty easy to get from one country to the other here," I observed to Maillard.

"Yes, we get along quite well, especially because in our region of Switzerland, French is the spoken tongue, which makes us what you Americans call 'kindred spirits.'"

No more than a half hour had passed when we entered Évian, whose streets I recognized from my earlier visits. After a couple of turns down narrow and busy streets, Maillard pulled up to a solid stone structure with the words *Preféecture de Police* on the facade and beneath them, three tricolor flags spread above the front door.

We entered the building and at a table in the entrance hall encountered a dour, mustached functionary, probably the Gallic equivalent of a desk sergeant, whom Maillard spoke to in French. He nodded curtly, picked up a phone and dialed, speaking briefly into the mouthpiece and replying. Less than a minute later, a petite woman of perhaps thirty attired smartly in civilian clothes emerged from a hallway, smiled as if she meant it, and beckoned us to follow her.

We were shown into an anteroom, apparently her domain, and then were led to an inner sanctum, where we were greeted by a tall man resplendent in what we were to learn was a *commissaire's* uniform. "Ah, *mon ami*," he said to Maillard as they kissed each other on the cheeks. Our host then turned to us and said in English, "I am René Bouchard and I welcome you both." He held out a hand in an American-style greeting and we each shook it. Wolfe, no fan of shaking hands, realized it would be churlish—to use a favorite word of his—to spurn the gesture.

"I recognize you, monsieur," Bouchard said to Wolfe. "Some years back, your photograph was in the *Paris Herald* after you had solved a famous kidnapping case in New York."

"You are too kind," Wolfe responded.

"Please sit down," the *commissaire* said, gesturing all three of us to a coffee table in one corner. The paneled office was elegant and spacious, a far cry from Inspector Cramer's dingy and messy quarters on Centre Street in Lower Manhattan.

Just as we got seated, the woman who had ushered us in entered silently, carrying a silver tray with a coffee urn, a teapot, a creamer, four elegant cups, and croissants. "What may I serve you gentlemen?" she asked in accented English.

"*Merci*, Marie," Bouchard said. Wolfe and I chose coffee, while Maillard and Bouchard opted for tea. I was the only one who took a croissant. After Marie had served us and made her soundless exit, Bouchard cleared his throat as a prelude.

"I am happy both of you both were able to come this morning, along with my dear friend Émile. I have no doubt you both speak French, but if you do not mind, I would like to conduct this conversation in English, as I am trying to improve myself in that respect. Here in Haute-Savoie, we get so many English and American visitors to Évian and the ski resorts that your language is heard in public almost as much as French."

"Thank you for your hospitality, sir," Wolfe said. "You are most gracious and we realize we have much to learn about your region and its unique qualities."

Bouchard smiled. "I already understand from Émile that you both are here on a quest of a sort."

"We are indeed. The cousin of one of my employees back home disappeared and when he came to Geneva to seek him, he, too, has disappeared. This cousin is a longtime lake steamer captain."

"I also gather from Émile that you believe there may very well be a connection between these disappearances and possible smuggling."

Wolfe raised his shoulders and let them drop. "Such is my conjecture, sir. Although I may be amiss in my thinking, I have come to the conclusion, albeit tentative, that watches, or parts thereof, are being illegally transported from Switzerland into France."

"What do you mean by 'parts thereof'?" Bouchard asked.

"Through information we have received, some of it supplied by Mr. Maillard through his associates in the watchmaking realm, it appears that Swiss-made movements intended for watches are the contraband being moved across international borders, and very possibly in large numbers."

"I know very little about fine watches," Bouchard said, "but I am aware the innards of these timepieces are extremely small and also extremely valuable. Is this possible smuggling the reason Mr. Goodwin was here in Évian and identified a truck as the suspected vehicle for the transporting of watch movements?"

"Yes, we had gotten information from another lake steamer

crew member, who was killed after he had spoken to us," Wolfe said.

"Yes, I had learned about that murder, Mr. Wolfe. We are close enough to Geneva that we get news of their activities. Also, we exchange information with that city's police force, as well. And before I forget it, we checked on the license number of the truck Mr. Goodwin saw. It will not surprise you to learn that it was a vehicle that had been stolen a week earlier."

"The same thing often happens in the United States," Wolfe said. "An automobile used in a crime, perhaps as a getaway car, invariably turns out to have been stolen."

"I have always felt that we have much in common with American police," Bouchard remarked. "I am curious as to how you get along with your local law enforcement agencies in New York."

Wolfe chuckled, something of a rarity for him. "Let us say we have an inconsistent relationship."

"That can be said here as well. But unlike many of my colleagues who resent private investigators. I am not averse to their existence. They have their place and, in the past, I have found them to be useful. I feel it is important for you to know my position on this matter."

"I appreciate your candor, sir. Mr. Goodwin and I are not here to impede any investigations. Our primary aim, of course, is to locate two missing individuals, while you are understandably interested in uncovering a probable smuggling operation. It would appear that our goals are inextricably bound together. Especially because my employee is one of those missing."

"Very well stated, Mr. Wolfe. We will of course continue to investigate the smuggling. As Émile has surely told you, we received from the Geneva police a photograph of Mr. Bernard, which was then posted in this building. And as I believe you know, one of my men reported seeing him in a rural area just outside Évian."

"Yes," I piped up, "and I tromped around in that general area, but without success. I was hampered by my inability to speak French, although I'm not sure how much being a native speaker would have helped."

"Perhaps it would not have," Bouchard agreed. "In the wooded areas above Évian, both residents and the transients, such as campers and vagabonds, are notoriously secretive, as we have long found. And they speak many languages."

"On his visits to Haute-Savoie, Mr. Goodwin has remarked on a laxity on the part of French customs officials," Wolfe said in a change of subject.

Bouchard nodded, his face showing resignation. "That has long been the case. The customs operation is not under my jurisdiction but is run directly from Paris. However, I do have enough authority that I can strongly suggest stricter enforcement, especially as smuggling may well be involved. In the past, this particular crime has not been seen as an issue between our two countries. Before you leave, Mr. Wolfe, I would like to have your telephone number, as we likely will have occasion to speak again, perhaps on several occasions. And I will give you my direct line."

"Archie, you've always got a pen with you. Please get the *commissaire*'s telephone number." That's the great detective for you. Never be bothered with such mundane tasks as jotting down information when you've got somebody to do it for you.

CHAPTER 16

After Maillard dropped us back at the hotel, I stopped by Wolfe's room before going to my own and said as he settled into his chair, "Well, you sure seemed to make a good impression on that French cop. I wish your relationship with Inspector Cramer was that convivial."

"It is of course advantageous for us to be on good terms with Mr. Bouchard, but here is the stark reality: We are no closer to finding Fritz than we were when we arrived in Geneva."

"Point taken. At the moment, I am sorry to say that I have no plan."

"Nor do I, Archie, although assuming Mr. Bouchard follows through on his intent at getting French customs to be more thorough in their baggage searches, there may be a breakthrough in the smuggling case."

"Yeah, maybe," I said, but I really didn't believe it and I suspect Wolfe did not, either.

* * *

The next morning, I climbed out of bed dispirited, showered, shaved, and dressed. I went down the hall to Wolfe's room and the door was ajar. Knocking, I got a "Come in, Archie." He was seated at the wheeled room service table with breakfast, of course.

"I don't like to disturb you while you're eating. I'll come back in, say, a half hour," I told him.

"No, stay!" he barked, waving a fork at nothing in particular. "Minutes ago, I received a telephone call from Mr. Bouchard and there has been a development."

"Really?"

"Soon after we left Évian, he reached the French national customs headquarters in Paris and, so he told me, demanded—that is the word he said he used—*demanded* that the border personnel become more thorough in their searches of belongings of those entering the country at Évian."

"About time," I said.

"To Mr. Bouchard's surprise, as he told me, his demand got quick results."

"You have my full attention."

"Early yesterday evening, a male passenger getting off a lake steamer at Évian endured a thorough search under the new program just instituted and in the satchel that he was carrying customs agents found more than several dozen watch movements with a total value in the thousands of Swiss francs—and French francs as well. Under questioning, the man gave no plausible explanation for having them in his possession and is now being held at the local police headquarters. Mr. Bouchard plans to question him this morning and has invited us to be present."

"Nice of him. How do we get there?"

"The *commissaire* is sending a car, which should be here in twenty minutes. Have you eaten?"

"No, but maybe I will be offered coffee and a croissant again."

"That hardly constitutes a breakfast," Wolfe admonished.

"Agreed, but as someone once said, 'Desperate times call for desperate measures.'"

"That someone was Hippocrates, a Greek physician and philosopher who lived centuries before Christ and whose original quote has been paraphrased by many persons, now including you."

"Nice to know I have something in common with the ancient Greeks."

"That's stretching a point," Wolfe said, pulling his watch from his vest pocket and glaring at it. "We should be going downstairs."

Just as we stepped outside, a dark, unmarked sedan of a make unfamiliar to me eased to the curb and the driver, in police uniform, stepped out of the car, saying, "Messieurs Wolfe and Goodwin, correct?"

I sat next to the driver and once again, Wolfe had a back seat to himself as we pulled away. "Do you speak English?" I asked the driver.

"Some," he said, smiling, "not a lot."

"I'm curious as to the make of this car."

"Make?" he said, wrinkling his brow as we pulled smoothly away.

"Not a Mercedes?"

He laughed. "Oh, I see now, a *brand*. No, not Mercedes. This is a Renault."

"It rides very well," I said, bringing another smile from our chauffeur.

"It is Renault's largest sedan," the driver said proudly.

I swiveled to Wolfe, who was grim-faced, obviously frustrated by the lack of a hand strap for him to cling to. "It's really a short trip," I said as if to reassure him, but to no avail, as his frown only deepened.

When the Renault pulled up in front of Évian's police station, I jumped out and held the door for Wolfe, who still grimaced. Inside, the same desk sergeant, if indeed that was his title, threw us a curt nod and picked up his phone, dialing. Seconds later, the petite Marie appeared and greeted us with a smile that likely quickened the heartbeats of young Frenchmen—and maybe older ones as well.

"So nice to see you gentlemen again," she said. "Please come with me."

We ended up back in Bouchard's plush office, where he looked up from behind his glass-topped desk, then stood, ramrod straight, to acknowledge us.

"Once again, thank you both for honoring us with your presence," he said. "Mr. Wolfe, you, I, and one of my lieutenants will be in the interview room with the man who has been in custody since yesterday. He gives his name as Charles Moreau and his papers confirm that.

"Mr. Goodwin, I am aware you do not speak French, so you and Marie Laval will be in an adjoining room with one-way glass and you will be able to hear our conversation. She has offered to translate for you."

"Thanks for having her help me," I said as Marie directed me to where we would observe the proceedings. "Mr. Goodwin, would you like coffee and some croissants?" she asked.

"You read my mind. I missed breakfast this morning."

She conveyed her sympathy with an expression of pity and slipped out, returning no more than two minutes later with a coffeepot, cups, cream, sugar, and several croissants in a basket. I felt better already.

We got ourselves seated close to the one-way glass and

watched as the participants filed into the unadorned interview room. A shuffling Charles Moreau, thin almost to the point of emaciation and clad in what I assumed to be a beige prison suit, wore a scowl that looked to be permanently pasted on his unshaven face. He was led in by the lieutenant, who I learned was named Allard.

Wolfe and Bouchard completed the cast of characters, with my boss eyeing his chair without enthusiasm and, sighing, wedged himself into it. The setup: Wolfe and Bouchard sat on one side of the square table, with Lieutenant Allard and Moreau on the opposite side. From here on, I will do my best to report on what was said, using Marie's translations and my memory.

Allard: Those present are: Commissaire René Bouchard; Private Investigator Mr. Nero Wolfe; Monsieur Charles Moreau; and Lieutenant Pierre Allard. This interview is starting at (Allard gave the time and date) and it is being tape-recorded.

Bouchard: Thank you, Lieutenant. Mr. Moreau, do you confirm that you have consented to this interview without legal representation?

Moreau: I am guilty of nothing so have no need for a lawyer.

Bouchard: What is your line of work, Monsieur Moreau?

Moreau: I am employed as a tram driver in Geneva and I have held that position for eight years.

Bouchard: Yesterday afternoon, you were detained in Évian after leaving a steamer from Geneva. A customs official, searching your belongings, found watch movements, with a total value estimated at 155,000 francs. Do you deny carrying these movements?

Moreau: I have no idea how those got into my satchel.

Wolfe: What reason did you have yesterday for going to Évian?

Moreau: I have friends here.

Bouchard: What are their names?

Moreau: That is no one's business but my own.

Wolfe: Come, come, sir. You have been detained for carrying a valuable commodity across an international border and you are hardly in a position to talk about your right to privacy.

Moreau: Who are you, anyway? You don't even sound French to me by your accent.

Bouchard: Mr. Wolfe is here at my express invitation and you are in no position to question his presence. In fact, you are in no position to question *anything* whatever. We are the ones asking the questions here.

Wolfe: Are you in the habit of carrying a satchel without checking its contents?

Moreau: Why should I bother to?

Bouchard: You do not seem to understand how weak your position in, Monsieur Moreau. We are in the process of checking to see if you have a criminal record and we expect the results soon. (As if on cue, a uniformed policeman entered the room and handed a sheet of paper to Bouchard.)

Bouchard (scanning the paper): I see that you were charged with smuggling stolen jewelry from Geneva to Évian eight months ago.

Moreau: That case was thrown out of court!

Bouchard: It was, but only because the plaintiff, a Geneva jewelry store proprietor, refused to appear. And why was that?

Moreau: How would I know?

Bouchard (to Allard): Check with the Geneva police as to why the jeweler did not come to Évian to testify. You can find his name in the court records.

Moreau: You can't just keep me here!

Bouchard: Yes, we can, and indefinitely, as you have been charged with cross-border smuggling, which is a crime of an international nature. Mr. Wolfe, do you have anything to add?

Wolfe: A question for Mr. Moreau: Is your employer at the tram company aware of your earlier court appearance?

Moreau: I . . . don't know.

Wolfe: Which is another way of saying he has no knowledge of that event. If you are indeed still a salaried employee of that company, Mr. Moreau, no doubt your superiors will begin to wonder what has become of you. (At this point, Morreau began to show signs of panic, looking with desperation at Bouchard, who pointedly avoided him.)

Bouchard: Pierre, please see that Monsieur Moreau is

returned to his cell. And make sure he is well fed during his visit with us.

The lieutenant nodded his obedience as he led a scowling Moreau out.

Back in the *commissionaire*'s office, Bouchard told Wolfe, "Allard will find out what the Geneva police know about why the jeweler did not testify in the Moreau trial."

"That would be helpful. It is likely that Mr. Goodwin and I will visit the jeweler." I am always happy to learn what Wolfe has planned for me and I often find out these plans while we are in the company of others.

We said our goodbyes to Bouchard and I thanked Marie for all her help before we climbed into the police sedan and were driven back to Geneva.

The next morning, I paid my usual visit to Wolfe's room and found him starting breakfast. "Good morning, Archie, I hope you slept well. I just received a call from Mr. Bouchard and his lieutenant has been busy. The Geneva police told him the jewelry store owner in question, a Claude Gervais, had declined to press charges against Charles Moreau and gave no reason for his decision."

"Then there was nothing that the Geneva cops could do, right?"

"Correct. As I had suggested earlier, we will go to the store, which is called Suisse Bijouterie, and speak to the proprietor."

"Pretty fancy name, but then, I'm sure the shop and its prices live up to that moniker." I went to the coffee shop, ordering my own breakfast, and a half hour later, Wolfe and I were in front of the hotel, where the doorman waved a taxi over.

"Suisse Bijouterie," I said to the cabbie, getting a nod from him as we lurched away from the curb, causing Wolfe to flinch. Maybe all this dashing around of late in various vehicles will give him a better appreciation of my own driving.

The store in question stood proudly on a bustling commercial avenue of sidewalk cafés, women's shops, bakeries, and beauty salons. The shop window was filled with a tasteful array of sparkling baubles, rings, and necklaces that looked like they had just been polished.

We stepped inside as the street clamor receded behind us. "*Bonjour*," a pinstripe-clad, silver-haired man said from behind a counter. If he was surprised by Wolfe's appearance, he did not show it.

"*Bonjour*," Wolfe replied, continuing in French until the man cut him off, saying "I sense that you are an English speaker."

"We both are," Wolfe responded.

"I am happy to converse in your native tongue. We get many British and Americans here and I like to sharpen my language skills when I can," he said with a salesman's smile, shooting his cuffs.

"Very well. I have occasion to travel to Geneva from time to time," Wolfe improvised, "and your shop has been recommended to me. However, I learned from an acquaintance that valuable jewelry had been stolen from you in the recent past, which concerns me. Are you the proprietor?"

"I am the owner—Claude Gervais, at your service," he said with a slight bow. "It is true that we did have a burglary here, at a time when the shop was closed. But we are fully insured."

"That is good to know," Wolfe said. "Were the perpetrators apprehended?"

Gervais looked uneasy. "Yes, they . . . he . . . was caught."

"And put on trial, I assume?"

"Uh, well, I chose not to press charges."

"Why is that, Mr. Gervais?"

"Well . . . I did not want to bring any more negative publicity to the shop. It was bad enough to have the newspaper stories about the burglary. If I may inquire, are you here as a customer, sir?" Gervais asked.

"I must confess, sir, that I am not. I am with a highly confidential international organization seeking to ensure that criminals face justice and your incident has been brought to our attention. I am here to inform you that the statute of limitations has not expired and that you can still press charges against the individual who so brazenly took priceless merchandise from your establishment. If you need legal help in this instance, our organization would be willing to help."

Wolfe then reached into the breast pocket of his suitcoat and pulled out a sheet of paper. "Mr. Gervais, I have here a form for you to sign so that our people can begin the process of a retrial." He held out a sheet and Gervais recoiled, as if Wolfe were holding a sprig of poison ivy.

"No, no! I want nothing to do with this," he said in a suddenly high-pitched voice. "Please go!"

"Very well," Wolfe said with a sigh, turning to me. "We have tried our best."

Once outside, I looked back and saw relief in Gervais's face. "That suave veneer of his sure crumbled quickly," I told Wolfe.

"As I had expected," he replied. "The man is terrified."

"And now you have added to that terror. You put on quite a show back there with that spiel about an international legal outfit. Very cute. I am supposed to be the man of action on this team, but from now on, you should leave the brownstone more often and prowl the dark streets of Manhattan with me. You could even pack heat. By the way, what was that paper that you pulled out of your pocket?"

"A blank sheet of hotel stationery."

"I will be damned. Didn't you think that Gervais would call your bluff at some point?"

"Not for a moment. As I said before, I knew the man was terrified."

"Of whom?" I asked.

"Years ago, you would have asked 'of who?'" Wolfe said. "There is hope for you yet."

"Gee, thanks, boss. But you still haven't answered my question."

"I don't know with certainty who the source of the terror is, but that is one of our goals—along with finding Fritz."

CHAPTER 17

The next morning when I made my post-breakfast stop in Wolfe's room, he put through a call to Bouchard in Évian.

"Good morning, sir," he said, holding the instrument away from his ear so I could hear the full conversation. "I have a question and I hope you will not think it to be impertinent."

"I will decide that after I have heard your question," the *commissaire* replied evenly.

"That is eminently fair, sir. How competent do you feel your men are in tailing a subject?"

"An interesting question, Mr. Wolfe. Of those at my disposal, I believe three—no, make that four—of them are what I would might skilled at following an individual without being detected. I suspect you have a reason for asking."

"You have seen through me, sir," Wolfe said with a chuckle. "I suggest—and it is only a suggestion—that you free Mr. Moreau from your bastille."

"Aha, I suspected that," Bouchard said, emitting his own version of a chuckle. "You feel our Mr. Moreau will lead the mouse to the cheese, no?"

"Nicely put. I concede this is a gamble, but it would seem that whoever gave him those watch movements to carry into France will be intensely interested in what has become of him—and of course of the movements as well."

"At this point, I must be candid," Bouchard said. "I do feel these men of mine are good at what you might call 'tailing,' but in truth, no one of them has had extensive experience. However, there was a situation when one of my gendarmes trailed a pickpocket for three kilometers to discover where he lived. It turned out that this man's abode also was home to a den of thieves that we had been hunting for weeks and we rounded up a whole crew."

"Let us hope this effort will be equally successful," Wolfe commented as the call was ended.

"I'm worried that Moreau will pick up any tails that get put on him," I said to Wolfe.

"I am not, Archie. This man, like our jeweler, lives in terror and once he is released from confinement he will be hell-bent upon trying to clear himself in the eyes of his employers. This fear will overcome any sense of his being under surveillance."

"I hope you're right."

"I understand that predictions are always risky, but mine in this instance is that we will be hearing from the *commissaire* within the next few hours."

We heard from Bouchard that afternoon, but not with the sort of news we had been expecting. When his call came, Wolfe and I were playing gin rummy in his room. Not normally a fan of card games, he had been taught gin rummy by an expert instructor,

Saul Panzer, and he soon became proficient at it to the point where he had already taken me for seven bucks when the telephone interrupted us.

"Yes, Mr. Bouchard . . . I see," Wolfe said, his face set in a frown as he held the receiver away from his ear. "Mr. Goodwin is with me. Please start again from the beginning if you will."

"As planned, our men were in place when we released Moreau."

"Was he surprised to be set free?"

"Not really. He is arrogant by nature and he acts as if he has been treated unjustly. 'It's about time' was his lone comment when he marched out of the station with a sneer on his face."

"And then. . . ?" I put in.

"Moreau walked to the nearest phone box, perhaps a block away, placing a call. About twenty minutes later, a gray Citroën sedan with two people inside picked him up."

"Were your men able to follow?" Wolfe asked.

"Yes, we had been well prepared, both on foot and with a car. The Citroën drove for perhaps ten kilometers up into the wooded foothills of Mont Blanc, with our car following. Although by now, it was obvious to them that we were in pursuit.

"The destination," Bouchard continued, "was a two-story chalet-style house in a clearing. The three from the Citroën went inside and our men waited two or three minutes, then knocked on the door and were admitted.

"They identified themselves as policemen and found the three recent arrivals and two other men preparing a meal. Our officers questioned them all and could not find a valid reason to make any arrests. These five all said they were itinerant laborers in search of work, which is not unusual in that area, where many day laborers are hired by logging companies and road maintenance crews."

"Did your men search the premises?" Wolfe asked.

"No, as we did not have the proper papers. But the interior seemed to be well maintained and if there were any weapons they were not visible."

"Was Mr. Moreau questioned?"

"He was and he accused our men of harassment, as no charge has been leveled against him."

"Archie and I would like to see this area."

"This is police business, Mr. Wolfe," Bouchard said in a firm tone.

"I am well aware of that. But the sole reason for our trip here from the United States was to locate my employee Mr. Brenner and his cousin. It remains likely that they could be in the vicinity, either in hiding or being held hostage."

"I suppose it is possible, Mr. Wolfe, but we cannot put you and Mr. Goodwin, as private citizens, in jeopardy."

"I must remind you, sir, that without my suggestion that you release Mr. Moreau, you would not know the location of what could be the headquarters of a smuggling ring and perhaps also the lair of at least one murderer, the killer of Lucien Leclerc in Geneva."

A long silence followed before the *commissaire* spoke. "Very well, I will send a car for you. But you must regard this as an ongoing investigation."

"I fully comprehend that."

"It's good that you understand, Mr. Wolfe. A car will be dispatched to pick you up in Geneva in the next few minutes."

I went back to my room and strapped on my shoulder holster, tucking my trusty Marley into it and donning the zippered jacket that showed no telltale bulges. Going back to Wolfe's room, I got a surprise: He had changed into slacks and a fleece-lined jacket and was in the process of tucking a Beretta .25 into his belt. He had bought the gun several years earlier after he had been attacked in his office by any angry client, who I had subdued. To my knowledge, the Beretta had never been fired.

When the car came for us from Évian, we climbed in and rode in silence, lost in the thoughts of what lay ahead. We had come here seeking answers to Fritz's fate in Switzerland, but it appeared those answers would be found in France.

At police headquarters, we were ushered into Bouchard's office, where he sat grimly behind his desk. "What is the present situation?" Wolfe asked as we sat.

The *commissaire* leaned back and clasped his hands behind his head. "I have briefed my superiors in Chamonix as to the situation and their orders are that we continue to monitor the activities at the chalet. They want to avoid any chance of violence."

"There already has been violence—the killing of Monsieur Leclerc," Wolfe said.

"But we do not know the source of that violence. The perpetrator may well be in Switzerland, not here."

I have seen Wolfe frustrated before, so I know all the signs: clenched teeth, the opening and closing of fists, and shortened breaths. "Sir, it appears we are at an impasse. All I ask is for us to see the place where Mr. Moreau is now ensconced."

Bouchard sighed. "We are in the process of posting men around the perimeter of their stronghold, if it can be termed as such. And to what end?"

"To satisfy my curiosity. You claim to be impressed by my work in America. Humor me in this situation."

"You are wearing me down and I appreciate that much of your concern is for the safety of Monsieur Brenner and his cousin. All right, one of my gendarmes will drive you to the site and perhaps that will give you some idea as to how we might proceed. But . . . my man has orders that under no circumstance are you or Mr. Goodwin to leave the automobile. Is that understood?"

"It is," Wolfe replied.

Bouchard had a gendarme brought into his office and he made the introductions and then spoke in French to the man who was to be our driver. Wolfe later translated: "These are Mr. Wolfe and Mr. Goodwin. You are to drive them to the place we are keeping under surveillance. They realize they have orders to stay in the automobile at all times." The officer clicked his heels, nodded smartly, and we were off.

With Wolfe and me in the back seat of the unmarked police sedan, the gendarme steered through the streets of Évian and then into sparsely populated areas that eventually gave way to stands of pines and the occasional small house or shack. This was similar to the terrain I had hiked through earlier on my fruitless search. The car's engine whined as we climbed higher through the woods and finally came to a halt in a clearing, some fifty yards from the two-story chalet Bouchard had described earlier.

"That is it," our driver said in fractured English, pointing at the house with a nicotine-stained finger. We gazed at it for perhaps a half minute and then Wolfe told the gendarme in French that he could return to headquarters.

CHAPTER 18

After yet another gendarme had driven us back to Geneva, Wolfe and I went into the hotel, where he suggested we have a drink. As we sat at a table in the lobby bar, Wolfe with a beer and me a scotch and water, I said, "The cops here are not big on action, are they?"

"They are cautious to a fault and Mr. Bouchard seems overly in awe of his superiors."

"I'll say. He was hesitant about even taking us to where Moreau is now."

"You noticed it, of course," Wolfe stated.

"Of course."

"Do you have any doubt?"

"None whatever."

"Could you find your way back there? And at night?"

"Yes, with my eyes closed—okay, maybe that's a slight exaggeration."

"Can we get a car?"

"Yes, easily. I assume we're talking about renting one, with me behind the wheel?"

"I am."

"It should be easy to get a car in the heart of a busy city."

"After breakfast?"

"You're certainly filled with questions today. Yes, I'll find out where the rental agencies are and take a cab."

"Satisfactory."

The next morning after eating in the coffee shop, I got names of car rental agencies at the front desk and hopped a taxi into the center of the city.

After showing my passport and driver's license to a red-jacketed woman behind the counter, I filled out the paperwork for a Mercedes sedan, figuring Wolfe would expect to be chauffeured in style. Besides, I had already seen plenty of Mercedes on the streets of both Geneva and Évian and I didn't want us to stand out in something like a Bentley, which also was available. Next, I drove to a camping and outdoor store and bought two flashlights, or "torches," as they are called, a coil of strong rope, and a Swiss Army knife.

I was on edge for the rest of the day, as is usually the case when we're nearing the defining moment in a case. This is different, though, as there would not be one of "those damned charades," as Inspector Cramer liked to call the sessions where Wolfe gets all the suspects into the brownstone so that he can divulge the identity of the guilty party or parties. In this case, we already knew who those individuals were, although not by name.

We left the hotel after an early dinner, driving in the gathering twilight, and I am happy to say that our experience at the French border was uneventful. A polite customs man cast a flashlight around the car's interior, had me open the trunk, which was empty, and then waved us on.

Once we were in Évian, now enveloped in total darkness, and with rain falling almost sideways, accompanied by thunder and lightning, my sense of direction kicked in and I was able to navigate the narrow streets that led toward our destination, aided by the windshield wipers. I parked the Mercedes on the side of an unpaved road several hundred feet from the chalet we had seen earlier. At the moment, however, it was not that building that interested us but rather a smaller single-floor house behind it and slightly above it on one of the hills that sloped upward toward Mont Blanc. Both Wolfe and I had taken note of the unimpressive building on our earlier visit.

Lights shown in the covered windows of both structures as we moved toward the smaller one, with me carrying a looped coil of rope over my shoulder. I have noted before that despite his girth, Nero Wolfe is surprisingly agile and light-footed. Such was the case this night, as he moved silently forward on the balls of his feet. Up to this point, our flashlights had remained off so as not to attract attention.

With rain pelting us as the electrical storm intensified, I crept to a window that had slightly parted curtains and, peering in, saw a tableau I hope never again to encounter. Three people occupied a sparsely furnished, shadowy room lit only by a floor lamp with a low-wattage bulb.

A scruffy man in his thirties slouched in a chair with a revolver beside him and a scowl on his unshaven face. The second individual, clad in slacks and a torn shirt and with a blackened eye was . . . Fritz Brenner. The third party, also shabbily dressed and with bruises on his face, was almost surely Fritz's cousin Paul Bernard, although I had never seen the man.

Wolfe moved beside me to the window and his reaction to the scene was a low growl, almost guttural in nature. Because we have worked together for so long, no words were exchanged, but we knew what we would do next.

I gently tried the door to the small house and to my surprise, it opened. Any noise I made was covered by the storm, which had grown in intensity, and we both moved into a small entryway. Fate intervened when I stepped on a squeaky floorboard at an instant when the thunder stopped briefly, alerting the man with the revolver.

He jumped up, grasping the pistol in both hands and swinging it in an arc toward the door, barking *"Qui est là?"* which I later learned was "Who is there?"

Wolfe surprised me by using his bulk to muscle his way into the room, firing his Beretta once. The shot hit the mark, its target clutching his either forearm or chest, screaming and writhing. The weapon dropped to the floor as Fritz and Paul Bernard jumped up, their expressions registering a mixture of shock and relief.

While their captor struggled to recover and get to his feet, I stepped in and ran a fist into his midsection, doubling him over as he retched. He fell to the floor in agony as I took lengths of the rope, cutting them with the Swiss Army knife and tying his hands behind his back and his ankles together, ignoring his cries. I did not feel cold-hearted in the least.

"Now we've got to get out of here, fast!" I barked, responding to Fritz's plea that he had to get his bag from the other room, presumably the bedroom.

"No time, the shot might have been heard. Keep your gun drawn; we might need it to save our skins," I yelled to Wolfe, gripping my own Marley. Then the four of us slipped out into the torrential rain and thunder. Lady luck apparently was on our side, as no movement came from the chalet fifty yards below us.

With me in the lead and Wolfe bringing up the rear, we made our way through the woods with both Fritz and Bernard struggling to keep up amid groans and painting. God knows what they had been through.

We made our way to the car without incident, with Wolfe sitting beside me in front and the two just-released captives in the back seat. Fritz kept thanking us and saying, "I thought we were going to die" over and over.

"What about the man we left back there?" Wolfe asked as we pulled away.

"What about him?"

"Archie, I shot him. He could die."

"Doubtful, you probably just winged him," I said. "Somebody from the big house will come and relieve him soon. They probably stand guard in shifts."

"You don't know that."

"Not to a moral certainty, I don't. Look. Here's what we can do if you're worried about a low-life who would just as soon shoot you as look at you. We'll stop at a phone box along Évian's main drag and you can call the police number—I've got it in my notebook—disguise your voice, and tell whoever answers that there's been a shooting in a small house up in the hills behind a large chalet."

"We don't have the address," Wolfe complained, clearly upset at having plugged someone.

"Screw the address, if there even is one up in those damned boondocks. The police figure to know the place. After all, they took us there themselves."

"So, it is highly likely that they will know that we—I—did the shooting," Wolfe complained.

I shrugged. "No reason they will. After all, the men in that house are questionable to begin with. Seems like a shooting in their outbuilding would hardly be surprising."

Wolfe looked uncomfortable and I realized our normal roles had been reversed. I'm usually demanding some sort of action while Wolfe is the one who invariably counsels patience.

We drove in silence for several minutes until he said in exasperation, "All right, we will locate a telephone. Give me the number and money and I will call the police."

That's Wolfe for you. He never carries cash, be it bills or coins, thinking that money is beneath him. We found a phone box and I started to fish coins out of my pocket before realizing they were Swiss, not French, and I cursed.

At this point, Fritz piped up: "Mr. Wolfe, French telephones don't take coins, they use *jetons*. Here, take one. I got these from a post office here when I felt I might need to make calls." He handed Wolfe a small disc.

I then gave Wolfe the police number. With the jetton, he wedged his way into the enclosure, made the call, and returned to the car, grumbling.

"All right, are you happy, now?" he muttered.

"I should be asking you that question," I shot back. "After all, you're the one who insisted we do this."

We made it through customs back into Switzerland, although the guard at the border cast a questioning glance at our back seat passengers, then looked at me with raised eyebrows. "They had too much to drink," I told him and he knew enough English to shake his head and smirk before waving us on into his country.

As we approached Geneva, Wolfe swiveled toward Fritz. "I have been a ninny. I should have asked this immediately: Do you need medical treatment?"

"No, sir, not at all. I am perfectly fine, just tired."

"What about you?" he asked Paul Bernard.

"I also am all right, mostly hungry."

"We can easily rectify that problem," Wolfe said. And to Fritz: "You are going to require clothes, as your things got left behind back in Évian."

"No, sir, most of the clothing I brought here is still back in Mr. Maillard's house."

"Well, one thing is of immediate need. You both need to get cleaned up."

"This can be done at my home," Bernard said, "and I will loan Fritz something to wear until he can get to Mr. Maillard's house."

I drove the Mercedes to Bernard's flat and we waited in the car for the pair to make themselves presentable. "They have been through a lot," I said to Wolfe.

"We will learn more later," he replied. "They both appear underfed, so we need to deal with that issue before we can get Fritz back to Mr. Maillard's. Do you agree?"

"Absolutely and, although my advice has not been solicited, my suggestion is to get them fed without grilling them about all that they've been through. That can come later."

When Fritz and Paul Bernard came down to the car, they looked much better, having shaved and with neatly combed hair. "Now for a meal," Wolfe said. "We will go to our hotel and dine in my room." Neither man complained.

When we entered the hotel, we were intercepted by the desk clerk. "Ah, Monsieur Wolfe," he said. "A gentleman has tried several times to reach you. Here is his name," he said, handing Wolfe a sheet of paper.

"I expected this," he told me after looking at it. "Our French *commissaire*, Mr. Bouchard, has telephoned me three times. What do you suppose he wants?"

"I can't imagine," I said in the straightest face I could muster. "You will have to find out."

"Later. Now to dinner."

When we got to Wolfe's quarters, I gave the men the room service menu and, at Wolfe's instructions, I told them, "Order whatever you wish. It's important that you both get your strength back, given what you've been through."

After they decided on their meals and Wolfe and I made our own selections, I called the orders downstairs, requesting that a larger room service table also be brought up along with two extra chairs. Fortunately, Wolfe's room was big enough to accommodate all of this.

We ate in a somber silence, with Wolfe attempting to start a conversation about the history of Switzerland's neutrality, but there was little enthusiasm for the subject, other than my occasional somewhat lame contributions. Fritz seemed particularly uneasy and I knew why: For years, he had been used to cooking for and serving Nero Wolfe and now the shoe was on the other foot, so to speak. He was the one being served and catered to and he was at a loss as to how to handle the situation.

After we all had finished, Wolfe pushed back from the table and said, "If you excuse me, I need to make a telephone call. Please stay where you are."

He dialed the number Bouchard had left and held the receiver away from his ear for my benefit. "I have been trying to reach you, Mr. Wolfe," the *commissaire* said with an edge in his voice.

"I was unavailable for some time. You now have my attention, sir."

"There has been a shooting in the hills above Évian in the very location that you had been driven to earlier. We received word by telephone from an anonymous caller."

"Indeed? Was anyone injured?"

"Yes, one man was hit, but not mortally. He was found by our man, tied up and conscious."

"Do you have any clue as to the identity of the shooter?" Wolfe asked.

"None at all. And the injured man—his papers identified him as Henri Duval, an itinerant laborer—has refused to answer any of our questions. He has been taken to a hospital.

"We also talked to people, all men, who appear to be living in the larger adjoining house and none of them acted as if they even knew Duval. We didn't believe them, of course, and they denied any knowledge of what the smaller house was used for, or that they were even aware of its existence. In that rural region, it is common for people to live as what you might call 'squatters' in houses and cabins. Most are not law-breakers, but some have been known to cause minor trouble."

"As you know, I had been curious about that chalet."

"We have been too, Mr. Wolfe, but we have nothing that we are as yet able to prove. Have you received any news concerning your employee's whereabouts?"

"Oh yes—I should have immediately mentioned that," Wolfe said. "Both my colleague and his cousin have just appeared in Geneva, apparently unharmed, and Mr. Goodwin and I are about to learn the reason for their disappearance."

"That is very interesting," the *commissaire* said, "very interesting. I am curious as to what you will discover about their difficulties."

"You will be hearing from us, sir," Wolfe said, ending the call.

"You lie with the best of them," I said out of the hearing of Fritz and Paul Bernard. "Put me down as impressed."

"You should not be, Archie. I suspect Mr. Bouchard did not buy my story. Like me, he surely looks askance at coincidences."

"Good point. What's next?"

"Let us now hear from Fritz and his cousin."

CHAPTER 19

I had room service take away the dinner table but I kept the extra chairs. Wolfe settled into the room's one comfortable (for him) chair and I made a seating semi-circle for the four of us.

"Gentlemen, please be seated," Wolfe said, "and we shall begin. Mr. Bernard, tell us how your difficulties began."

Paul Bernard cleared his throat and began, albeit haltingly. "I will speak in English . . . if you do not mind. Being a captain on a lake steamer and meeting many people . . . I find it helpful to learn several languages and we have so many riders from England, Canada, and the United States."

"Use whatever tongue is most comfortable," Wolfe said.

Another throat-clearing. "A few weeks ago, I began to notice passengers—all of them men—who seemed to be acting . . . is *secretive* the right word?"

"It very well could be applicable in this case. Go on."

"These men all boarded at Geneva, all carried canvas bags

slung over one shoulder, and all got off at Évian-les-Bains. At first, I thought nothing of this, but it continued until it was hard to ignore and I became most curious."

"Please go on," Wolfe prodded.

"I started sharing this concern with members of my crew. I told one of them, Lucien Leclerc, my first mate, about one of the men I was suspicious of. He became very interested in my concern, saying he would do some investigating of his own."

"Go on," Wolfe said, opting not to tell Bernard about Leclerc's fate until later.

"I am not one to be intimidated," he continued. "I always have run my steamer as a tough but fair captain who speaks his mind. And so it was with this business. I had a sense that something was wrong and I was not afraid to say so. I wanted my crew to be alert to anything illegal that might be happening and word must have got out that I was doing some investigating."

"How trusting are you regarding your crew?" Wolfe asked.

"Perhaps more than I should be," Bernard conceded. "I like to think that I know my men, but some of them have only been with us a short time. And it is possible that at least one had been planted on the boat to aid those who apparently were smuggling goods."

"Or that so-called plant may have been put there to keep an eye on you," I said. "How careful are you or the steamer company in the hiring of new crew members?"

"The head office usually does the formal hiring, although I usually also talk to every new hand, just to get a feeling for what kind of person he is."

"Did any recent additions to the crew make you uneasy?" I asked.

Bernard shrugged. "Nothing I could identify. You have to remember that a lot of those who sign on to vessels of any kind tend to be tough and hard and are often heavy drinkers as well."

"And they all probably have tattoos of their girlfriends' names on their chests or arms," I said to lighten the conversation.

That got a rueful smile in response. "Yes, there are plenty of tattoos, no question."

"Mr. Bernard, if you were unaware of this because you were indisposed, you need to know that Mr. Goodwin and I placed an advertisement in a Geneva newspaper seeking information on your whereabouts that included a photograph," Wolfe said.

"Really?" He jerked upright in surprise.

"We received two responses. One was from Mr. Leclerc and I regret to tell you that our conversation with him may have led, at least indirectly, to his death. The other was from a Geneva woman who had seen you in Évian in a verbal confrontation on the street with a man she described as having 'many tattoos on both of his arms that included hearts, crosses, and a lightning bolt, as well as an earring in one ear.' We would like to learn more about the identity of this colorful individual."

Paul Bernard put his head in his hands and moaned. "I am responsible for Lucien's death, just as much as if I had done the killing myself."

"You did not realize the kind of people you were dealing with," I told Bernard in an effort to ease his pain.

"Please continue," Wolfe prodded.

"The Geneva woman you spoke to is essentially accurate as to what she saw. The man I argued with is Carl Brauer, who had been a member of my crew until I let him go after about two months. The company does the hiring, as I said, but I have the authority to do the firing.

"Brauer was surly, almost from the start, and he seemed

overly interested in my suspicions about some of our passengers, particularly men leaving the steamer at Évian, although he never brought the subject up to me, and I never took him into my confidence. In addition to that, he constantly questioned my orders and didn't get along well with the others on the crew."

"How did Mr. Brauer react to his dismissal?" Wolfe asked.

"It will not surprise you to learn that he responded with anger, claiming I wasn't capable of captaining a garbage scow, let alone a lake steamer."

"What do you see as the cause of this man's animus?"

"That does puzzle me, Mr. Wolfe. As I said, he seemed hostile immediately and I did not give him any reason to be."

"What was the reason for your fracas in Évian?" I asked.

"I wasn't working that day and I rode one of our steamers there as a passenger because of my suspicions about those men with the canvas bags. I was walking along the street not far from where the steamers dock and Brauer shouted out to me, 'Why don't you stay on that your goddamned boat of yours?'

"I told Brauer to 'go somewhere and sober up,' and that enraged him even more. He started toward me with clenched fists as though getting ready to fight and then suddenly backed away and said something like 'you will regret even having met me,' to which I replied, 'Oh, I already have' and walked off in another direction. I guess I just had to have the last word," Bernard said.

"And you never saw Brauer again?" Wolfe posed.

"Yes and frankly I viewed him as just a harmless . . . how do you say it in English . . . *windbag*?"

"That word will nicely suffice, sir. Now Mr. Goodwin and I would like to hear how both of you ended up in your recent predicament. Do not spare any details, no matter how unimportant you believe them to be."

"Should I start, or would you prefer?" Paul Bernard asked Fritz.

"You go ahead and I will make contributions if and when I have something to add."

"All right. One day, or maybe it was two, after I had run into Brauer on the street, I was back in Évian, I began going into shops along the main avenues asking proprietors if they had seen anyone who they thought to be unusual or suspicious. As it turned out, that was a foolhardy thing to do."

"Did any of these shopkeepers respond to your queries?" Wolfe asked.

"No, although some of them looked at me strangely. If I were to guess, I would say they saw me as a *bavard,* which in English is. . . ? He looked around for help.

"A gossip or a busybody," Fritz said as Wolfe dipped his chin in agreement.

"Yes and I now realize that as I continued my questioning of merchants throughout the day, I was being marked as a . . . *busybody* by a certain group, as I was very soon to learn. Discouraged, I was about to go back to the dock and get a Geneva-bound steamer when an automobile pulled up beside me and a bearded man wearing a beret jumped out and yelled 'Get in!' I turned my back on him and he hit me on the head with something hard—I never saw what it was—and he pushed me toward the open door to the back seat, where another man yanked me in.

"Once inside the car, I was grabbed and a sack got put over my head. I was worried that I would suffocate but it turned out I could still breathe, with some difficulty. I tried to yell but I got slapped in the head, hard, and was told to shut up. The car, with a man next to me and two in the front seat, drove off and went on bumpy roads for maybe thirty minutes, stopping at what I now know was the house where you found me, Mr. Wolfe."

"How long were you a prisoner in that house?" I asked.

"What day it this?" I told him.

"Then I was in there for . . . nineteen days. I did get away once and managed to run perhaps a couple of kilometers, but they chased after me and took me back to that . . . that *place*."

"Mr. Bernard, tell us how you were treated and what was said to you during that painful time," Wolfe questioned.

"At any given time, there was either one or two men guarding me with pistols. I got fed twice ever day and the place had a bathroom. When I asked why I was being held, they didn't answer except to tell me I should learn to mind my own business, or words like that.

"At first, I thought I was going surely to be killed, but as time went on, I had a little hope that I might survive. And then, as you both know, I was joined, much to my surprise, by Fritz, but that is his story." Bernard took a deep breath and leaned back, exhausted by his tale.

Wolfe turned to Fritz with eyebrows raised as the cue for him to begin. Clearly uncomfortable being the center of attention, he started slowly.

"I got to Geneva with no airplane problems . . . and, as was the plan, I went to Émile Maillard's house, where I stayed until . . . Oh, Mr. Wolfe, we need to call Mr. Maillard and tell him I am safe. I am sure he's concerned."

"We will, Fritz. Please continue."

"By accident or coincidence, I ended up following Paul's actions and with the same result! After I got settled at Émile Maillard's home, I went to the Geneva steamer docks and started asking about Paul. The only thing of consequence I learned was that he had seemed concerned about something that was going on in Évian-les-Bains. I took the lake steamer there, along with a photograph I had of Paul, and I began showing it to people on the street and in the shops.

"I got very little reaction from anyone I talked to other than shrugs, so after more than an hour, I was on the point of giving up when a car pulled up next to me and, similar to Paul's experience, I was grabbed. They tried to force me into the car and, when I resisted, started swearing at me in French—words I will not repeat.

"But I was unable to resist them and one man hit me with his fist, accounting for this swelling in my eye, which has begun to go down now."

"Other than the profanity, what did they say to you?" Wolfe asked.

"Very little, sir. Only that we were poking our noses into business that did not concern us. And like with Paul, they put something over my head and drove me to the place where you found us. I'm afraid neither of us would make very effective spies."

"Was your life in that house similar to what Mr. Bernard has described?"

"Yes, much the same. We were fed, but not very much, and what we ate was not very good. And, of course, our clothes were . . . well, you saw what we looked like when you found us." Fritz shook his head in a combination of disgust and shame.

"Fritz, do not concern yourself about your appearance when we found you. The important thing is that you are safe now." That is about as close as Wolfe comes to expressing emotion.

"Thank you. When you and Archie burst into the room, it was like something out of a motion picture."

"I will have to take your word for that," Wolfe said. "Did the men who held you prisoners say anything that indicated their purpose?"

"They barely spoke to us at all. At least one of them was in the house at all times and awake and they sometimes kept the outer door locked, I think. We only knew their names as Marco and Johnny."

"And it was obvious from the way they spoke that they were French," Paul Bernard said. "One had an accent that would place him in or near Marseille."

"Did you sense there were other men in the larger house?" Wolfe asked.

"Maybe, but the windows in our place were mostly covered so we couldn't see outside," Fritz said.

"But the way our jailors kept going in and out made it appear that they must be going to the other place," Bernard put in.

"How many men guarded you in the time you were there?" I asked.

"Just the two I named. The one Mr. Wolfe shot was Marco. Did he survive?"

"We think so," Wolfe said. "It does you honor to ask. Is there anything either of you can think to add about your unfortunate experience?"

Both men shook their heads. They looked like they could use some sleep.

CHAPTER 20

In the morning, Wolfe telephoned Maillard to let him know both Fritz and Bernard were safe and the enthusiastic response was that he would come to the hotel and take them home, Bernard to his residence and Fritz to Maillard's own house.

When Maillard stepped into the hotel lobby a half hour later, we all were there to meet him. "My heavens, it is so, so good to see you both safe," the restaurateur said with emotion as we gathered around a table in the coffee shop. "Please tell me how you are."

"There is plenty of time for that," Wolfe said, "as you will be with each of them in your role as their chauffeur. Have you discovered anything more of interest from your friends in the watchmaking business?"

"Not really, Mr. Wolfe, except that one of the smaller companies making watches seems to be having trouble getting movements from their supplier."

"What is the name of the watchmaker?"

"Deltona Timepieces, right here in Geneva. They are a much smaller operation than their competitors, the ones whose names you are familiar with, but they have begun to get a reputation for making a fine product."

"Do you happen to know who their owners and directors are?"

"I don't, but I can easily find out for you, probably quickly."

"That would be most helpful. Do they make their own movements?"

"I don't know, but given their size, I doubt it. Would you like me to find out who the supplier of their innards is?"

"Only at the risk of leaning too heavily upon your generosity."

"Nonsense. I am happy to do it. After all, I strongly suspect that you and your Mr. Goodwin had something to do with Messieurs. Brenner and Bernard being here with us now."

After the former detainees left with Émile Maillard, Wolfe and I had dinner in his room. By now, the hotel staff was getting used to hauling a wheeled table, food, and beverages up to our floor and then taking the table back down again. After all, Wolfe is a good tipper, using money from me.

The next morning after shaving and showering, I got to Wolfe's room with its door ajar just as he received a telephone call. "Yes, Mr. Maillard, I slept well and I trust you did as well. . . . Ah, that is very quick work indeed. Yes, I have a pen. Go ahead."

Wolfe wrote as Maillard was presumably giving him information. "Yes, I believe I have it all down, sir. Thank you for your efficiency. How is Fritz today?"

"He had a fine appetite this morning, which should answer your question."

"I am delighted to hear it. And again, thank you."

Wolfe showed me what he had written down. "That is very interesting," I said. "I would not have believed it."

"I had my suspicion," Wolfe replied, "but I was not totally sure. Archie, please telephone Commissaire Bouchard. I wish to speak to him."

Once again, I get to carry about the boss's orders, although I know damn well that he knows how to use that instrument developed by Mr. Bell. I got the front desk to put through the call.

"He answered, even at this hour," I said, handing Wolfe the instrument.

"How are you, sir?" Wolfe asked, holding the phone away from his ear for my benefit. He's all heart.

"Mr. Wolfe, it is very good to hear from you. Do you have something to tell me, perhaps about how your missing men came to be found?"

"I have no information about that, sir, but I do know something both interesting and troubling that is going on within your purview."

"Really?"

"Yes, sir. Very soon, if I am not mistaken, a facility within your Haute-Savoie region will begin producing a new brand of wristwatches. And these watches will be powered by movements that have been brought into France from Switzerland illegally."

"Mr. Wolfe, how have you come by this information?"

"That is not important at the moment. You oversee a competent and well-staffed police force, and that force should be able to locate this facility."

"Can you be more specific, sir?"

"If you are asking whether I know the precise location, the

answer is no. But I am confident that you command an army of highly trained officers who are aware of what transpires within your sphere."

"Is there anything more you can tell us about this supposed new watchmaking facility?"

"Not at present. But you may want to join forces with police in the Geneva area."

"Are you suggesting that they are aware of what you are calling a cross-border operation?"

"I am not, sir, because I have not been in communication with any law enforcement agencies in Switzerland."

"Mr. Wolfe, I am at a loss as to how to respond to what you are telling me."

"I don't see why, Commissaire. I have given you information I believe to be accurate."

"Very well. I may want to discuss this with you again."

"Until further notice, you can reach me in my hotel, sir." All that could be heard at the other end of the line was a sigh before the call ended.

"Let me guess what comes next," I said to Wolfe. "We make a visit to a certain establishment in the heart of Geneva."

"You are most perspicacious, Archie." He loves to throw words like that at me, and I made a mental note to look it up in a dictionary later, that is, if I could figure out how to spell it.

We got a taxi in front of our hotel and, after giving the cabbie the address, off we went. I had to mentally salute Wolfe for the way he was bearing up under having to be a passenger in both cabs and private cars driven by people he didn't know. He still tensed up, although he had gotten used to riding in vehicles that didn't have a strap he could grab hold of.

We pulled up at the curb in front of Suisse Bijouterie and we climbed out as I paid our driver. The nattily attired Claude

Gervais stood proudly behind the store's front counter just as he had on our earlier visit.

"Good morning, gentleman," he said, and his pasted-on smile quickly faded as he recognized us. "Er, is there anything I can do for you?"

"Possibly, sir," Wolfe answered. "When we were here earlier, my organization authorized me to urge you to press charges against the gentleman who burglarized you."

"I remember," Gervais said stiffly.

"When I reported your reluctance, my superiors asked me to return here and urge you to reconsider your decision."

"I am sorry, sir, but I believe I stated my position firmly on your previous visit. I stand by my earlier position."

"So be it," Wolfe said with a shrug and started to walk away, but stopped, peering into the display case. "Those are Deltona watches?" he asked.

"A superb brand," Gervais answered, clearly happy with the change in subject matter.

"Yes, I have heard good things about them, as I have some familiarity with watch brands."

"We have the exclusive rights to sell them in Geneva," the owner said with pride.

"That is quite an honor, sir, I salute you. May ask who manufactures their movements?"

"A supplier named MicroMetrics, which does fine work."

"Are they here in Geneva?"

"Yes, I am happy to say. Would you like to see some of the watches?"

"Not at the moment, but perhaps at a later time."

"Anything else I can do for you gentlemen?"

"As far as you know, sir, have the people at Deltona been happy with the movements they get from MicroMetrics?"

"I have heard nothing from them about that," Gervais answered, beads of sweat starting to form on his brow.

"Really? As the exclusive distributor of their products, I should think you would be concerned that they are happy with what is surely the most important component of their timepieces."

"If you have no further reason to be here, I must ask you both to leave," Gervais said in what I would call an uppity tone. I looked at Wolfe for instructions and got a slight nod in return. We left.

CHAPTER 21

"The guy still seems nervous to me, and afraid," I told Wolfe after we left the jewelry store.

"He has much of which to be afraid, Archie. I have an assignment for you."

"Gee, that's exciting, I'm bracing myself. Bring it on."

Wolfe glared at me. "Ever the clown. We will now go back to the hotel. After we are back there for an hour, I want you to return here and gaze into the jewelry store window. Make sure you are seen by Mr. Gervais. Then walk away for fifteen minutes and come back, look in the window, pull out your notepad, and begin scribbling in it while studying the items in the window. As before, make sure the proprietor sees you."

"Are we trying to drive him crazy?"

"We, or you, specifically, are giving him something to think about. Go away, have lunch or whatever diversions you find in the midst of Geneva, and go back to the shop window for a third time, again with pencil and notepad."

"What happens if he comes outside?"

"What indeed? You are breaking no laws, merely admiring the merchandise so tastefully displayed behind plate glass."

"He may call the police."

"I seriously doubt that. If he does happen to come out and demand an explanation for your behavior, as I suspect he might, do not give him my name but have him telephone our hotel and ask for my room by number."

"All right, armed with my pencil and paper, I will go forth to do battle."

I took Wolfe's suggestion and had a very pleasant light lunch consisting of a croque monsieur, fries, and a glass of milk outdoors at a sidewalk café two blocks from the shop. I would later report to Lily Rowan that the young women of Geneva dressed every bit as well as those she and I had seen some years before while sitting at a similar café in Paris.

Returning to my post, I saw that Mr. Gervais was with a female customer as they both bent over a counter studying what appeared to be a necklace.

When he saw me, the proprietor twitched and tried to remain calm in the presence of what appeared to be a potential customer. I continued peering at the goods on display as, inside, the two seemed to be in an earnest discussion. Finally, both parties smiled and Gervaise went about packaging up a purchase as money smoothly passed between the two. The buyer, a fortyish woman with a fine sense of style, stepped out gracefully onto the sidewalk and nodded to me as she passed. I returned the nod, adding a *bonjour*.

After she had moved down the busy avenue with her

purchase, Gervas came out, glaring. "Why are you here?" he demanded, in a voice low enough that pedestrians passing us paid no attention.

"Just admiring your presentation," I said. "Very tasteful. I observed that you just had a successful transaction. You must be most pleased. Congratulations."

"What is it that you want?"

I turned toward him and did my imitation of what I have learned is a "Gallic shrug," although we were not in France itself. "I was just passing by, Mr. Gervais."

"Just passing by—hah! You are harassing me."

"By admiring your store? I hardly think that classifies as harassment."

"I have already told your colleague—two times—that I am not going to press charges against the man who burglarized the shop. Why can't he just let that go?"

"I suggest you telephone him," I said. "He is at the Hotel Lac Leman, here is the room number," I said, handing him a piece of notepaper.

"What is his name?" Gervais demanded.

"I am sorry, but I am not authorized to give you that information."

He snatched the paper from my hand, turned on his heel, and marched back into his place of business without uttering a word, which was jake with me.

When I got back to the hotel and went up to Wolfe's room, the door of which was ajar, I found him in the one chair that could accommodate him, reading one of the books he had brought, with a glass of beer and a bottle on the table next to him.

"I trust you had lunch," I said.

"Adequate. Perhaps I could get the hotel to hire Fritz to work in their kitchen on a temporary basis."

"Dream on. Did you receive a call in my absence?"

"I did, from Mr. Gervais. He was very angry and he said that 'my flunky'—that's what he called you—has been a detriment to his business."

"Did you identify yourself?"

"No, I merely picked up the instrument and said, 'Yes?', sure that it was him, given the timing. He demanded to know my identity and I told him I go by many names."

"The old 'man of mystery' trick, eh? What did he say then?"

"He told me how you were 'lurking'—that is the word he used—in front of his establishment and he insisted I do something about you."

"I told him I was not responsible for your actions, that you are rash and impetuous. I suggested he report you to the police."

"Thanks for hanging me out to dry, boss."

"Come, Archie, Mr. Gervais is hardly in a position to press charges against a passerby who stops to look in his window and he said as much. 'Call the police?' was his reaction to my suggestion. 'And precisely what am I going to tell them? What if they came to investigate? How would it look for the store to have a police van pull up in front?'"

"Bad publicity is also the reason he used for not wanting to pursue the case against the thief who broke into his shop. It sounds like he's over a barrel. By the way, I resent that 'flunky' label."

Wolfe raised his shoulders an inch and let them drop in a shrug. "I have absolutely no control over the terminology used by others, however inappropriate it may be."

"Well, thanks for that, anyway. Do you want me to keep going back to stare into the jewelry store window? It's enjoyable to see a stuffed shirt deflated."

"I hate to spoil your fun, but let us leave Mr. Gervais alone for now. He seems sufficiently rattled and we have the luxury of time with which to frustrate him. For the present, I am hoping to hear from our police associate in Évian-les-Bains."

It turned out that Wolfe did hear from the *commissaire* later that afternoon, just after I had entered his room.

"Hello, Mr. Bouchard; do you have any news?"

"I do and I believe it will interest you," he said as Wolfe once again held the receiver slightly away from his ear for my benefit. As you suggested, a small watch factory has begun production in our small village of Samoëns."

"You have my full attention, sir."

"The new enterprise is named Altos Chronometers and their watches also bear the Altos name. These products are priced slightly below the leading Geneva brands but are still expensive."

"What else have you learned about the company?"

"Very little, although we know they have secured a license, which gives them a right to produce and sell their products."

"So, in the eyes of the law, the company operates legally?" Wolfe asked.

"That is true, unless something is discovered that would cause them to lose their license."

"What is the price of one of their watches?"

"I would have to check, but given the current exchange rate between the French franc and the United States dollar, it would be somewhere in the neighborhood of one hundred and fifty dollars."

"Far more than most people would pay for something strapped to their wrist," said the man who has carried a pocket watch in his vest all the years I had known him.

"That is true, Mr. Wolfe, although these new Altos models are competing with some of the great Swiss watch names. They are not charging quite as much as some of those famous brands, but they still must display good workmanship, which drives up the labor cost."

"Do you know anything about the movements in the Altos watches?"

Bouchard chuckled. "I know why you are asking. I of course wonder, as I am sure you do as well, if the innards of these new watches are among those that have been illegally brought into France from Switzerland."

"It has crossed my mind," Wolfe said dryly.

"Mr. Wolfe, you have been extremely helpful to us, which I appreciate. I propose that we—my department, that is—purchase an Altos watch and take it apart to study the movement and to compare it to one of those our men confiscated from Charles Moreau. I invite you and Mr. Goodwin to join us when this is done."

"From what I have learned about the complexity of watch movements, I believe it would be imperative that an expert in these movements be present to confirm any findings."

"Do you have someone to suggest, Mr. Wolfe?" the *commissaire* asked.

"Not at the moment, but I believe we can locate an individual in Geneva."

"I would be in your debt, sir, if that could be accomplished and with expeditiousness."

"Sir, I commend you on your use of English. We will try to act promptly."

After the call had ended, I turned to Wolfe. "Let me guess: You want me to telephone Émile Maillard and hand the instrument to you."

"That is not a guess, Archie. It is a conclusion based upon your acuity."

"Have it your way," I told him as I began the process of

putting through the call to Maillard's home. He answered on the second ring and I handed the phone to Wolfe.

"Hello, Mr. Maillard. I trust you are well," he said, once again holding the receiver slightly away from his ear.

"I am, sir, thank you for inquiring. If you are asking about Fritz, I am pleased to report that his appetite is returning, thanks at least in part to the staff in my restaurant, where he has been dining much of the time."

"That is good to know. I confess I now must impose upon you on another matter."

"I am at your service, Mr. Wolfe."

"I am seeking an expert on the inner workings of watches. Mr. Goodwin and I will be going to Évian and we would like this individual to accompany us to a meeting there."

"It sounds intriguing," Maillard said. "Because you have offered no details, I will refrain from asking. However, before I try to secure the use of an expert on delicate mechanisms, I do have three questions: first, how will this individual be compensated for his knowledge and time; second, when would he be needed; third, how long is this assignment be likely to take."

"All legitimate questions, which I will answer in reverse order," Wolfe responded. "The assignment will take no more than a day. The expert would be needed this week, possibly as early as tomorrow. As for compensation, I will be guided by his or his employer's demands."

"Very well," Maillard said. "I will put out my net, as a fisherman might say, and learn whether I get any bites."

"Colorfully phrased," Wolfe said. "We will await word from you."

CHAPTER 22

We did not have to wait long for a response from Émile Maillard. No more than an hour passed before he phoned Wolfe with the name of an individual who was willing to undertake the request. "His name is Charles Challard." Wolfe told me. "He has been employed by one of the largest of the Geneva watchmakers for thirty years and, so Mr. Maillard tells me, he is considered by his employers to be the finest craftsman in the watch business. Mr. Maillard said he would bring the man to the hotel tomorrow morning."

"I still have the Mercedes we've been renting, so I assume we will be driving Challard to Évian."

"Your assumption is correct. Also, he expects to be paid one hundred Swiss francs for his effort."

"I'll make another assumption, which is that I will be the one paying him, from the wads of money I have been carrying around."

Wolfe's response was a nod.

* * *

Maillard pulled up in front of the hotel at nine the next morning with his passenger, a short, stocky, fiftyish man with thick glasses and gray hair, carrying a satchel similar to the one Doc Vollmer back home lugs around on his house calls. I already had gotten the rental Mercedes from the hotel garage and had it waiting at the curb.

Maillard introduced Challard to us and I quickly learned that he couldn't speak a word of English. We shook hands with him and he and Wolfe climbed into the back seat, where they proceeded to talk in French as I drove through Geneva and on along the shore of the lake toward France.

In the last few days, I had driven more than I do in a month at home. And I seemed so much like a chauffeur that I felt I should be wearing a dark suit and a black, billed cap as the two men in the back seat talked on, oblivious to my presence. We passed without a problem into France, getting a smile and a salute from the uniformed customs guard and a half hour later, I eased the Mercedes to a stop in front of the Évian police headquarters.

Even before we entered the building, the *commissaire* appeared at the door, greeting Wolfe and Challard in French and sending a thin smile in my direction. We all went inside to a windowless meeting room where Challard made a production of opening his satchel and spreading a linen cloth on the tabletop, then carefully smoothing it. Next came a box from which he extracted tools that looked like they could belong to a locksmith or a safecracker and arrangement them neatly. Like a surgeon, the man was doing his prepping.

Commissaire Bouchard then played his part in the performance by producing a watch and a circular device, no more than two inches in diameter and containing several levers along with toothed wheels that I assumed to be gears. Challard nodded at the mechanism with approval and turned to the watch, which he popped open with the help of one of his small, tweezer-like devices. Using another of his microscopic tools, he gently extracted the innards from the watch and placed it next to its like number on the linen.

Next, he pressed a loupe to one eye and leaned close to the two movements, studying one, then the other, and nodding. This continued for about a minute. He finally looked at Bouchard and turned his palms up in what I assumed to be a *voila!* gesture.

The two men and Wolfe then leaned close to one another at the table and exchanged comments and nods, after which Challard in his orderly way began repacking his tools. After he had finished that task, Bouchard took him aside and asked questions, scribbling notes about his responses.

"What was our expert's conclusion?" I asked Wolfe as we moved away from the others.

"He said the two movements were made by the same manufacturer, MicroMetrics, in Geneva, a relatively new company. He also noted that the serial numbers of each of them indicated they were made in the same batch. Further, he said the movements are of an inferior nature and that they have a limited life span, far shorter than those in the watches of the major Swiss brands.

"I will now speak to M. Bouchard, while you take our expert to the car for the trip back to Geneva." I followed orders and also gave Challard one hundred francs, getting a curt nod and nothing more as my thanks.

It was only after we had dropped Challard off at his watch-making facility in Geneva and returned to the hotel that I asked Wolfe about his conversation with Bouchard.

"He is of course interested in investigating Alto Chronometers and I suggested he start by learning the identity of their chief executive."

"I have a suspicion that you know who it is," I told him.

"Perhaps, although I thought it best for him to conduct his own investigation. He appears to be a competent and diligent law officer."

"And one who thinks highly of you and values your expertise."

"He may have an elevated opinion of my abilities, based upon what he has read in the press, which as you are aware is given to exaggeration and hyperbole."

"Do you think Lon Cohen's articles on you and your cases in the *Gazette* are full of exaggeration? I always thought you approved of that coverage."

"Mr. Cohen is an accomplished journalist, but he also is a pragmatist, Archie. He realizes, even if he doesn't admit it to himself, that if he gives us favorable treatment in the *Gazette*'s pages, we will be more inclined to favor him with information allowing him and his paper to get what he calls 'scoops.'"

"Okay, point taken, but I still think Bouchard has a lot of respect for you and your acumen."

"'Acumen', is it? You have been delving into the dictionary again."

"I'm always trying to improve myself, as you have urged for years."

"It is good to know that my ministrations have not all been for naught."

"What is your plan now, or do you even have a plan?" I asked to change the subject.

"We wait to hear from Mr. Bouchard, if he ever calls. This is his show."

* * *

Bouchard did call and we did not have to wait for long: The *commissaire* telephoned later that afternoon with a request that Wolfe sit in on a discussion he would be having the next morning with the man in charge of Alto Chronometers, none other than . . . Claude Gervais.

"What do you plan to accomplish by having me present?" Wolfe asked. "I have no standing within the French legal system."

"I want you present as an . . . I'm looking for a word in English . . . as an *unbiased* observer and also as an adviser."

"Will my presence in any way jeopardize the proceedings? I have had occasion to meet Mr. Gervais and he will likely take issue with my appearance."

"Let him take issue. There's absolutely nothing he can do to prevent your being present. Also, he will have a lawyer with him. We are scheduled to meet at ten, in the same room where we met with Mr. Moreau. As before, Mr. Goodwin can watch the proceedings from the adjoining room with my secretary, Marie Laval, who as before will translate the conversation."

"That is very kind of you—and of Marie," I said to Bouchard, who then said to Wolfe, "Do you have any questions, sir?"

"No and I will only be an active part of the proceedings when asked for comments by you."

"And no doubt I will seek your counsel at some point. We will see you tomorrow."

The next day, after Wolfe had breakfast in his room and I made my usual morning visit to the coffee shop, I wheeled the Mercedes out of the hotel's parking garage and onto the road that would take us across the border into France and on to Évian-les-Bains, a now-familiar route.

We arrived at the police building fifteen minutes before the meeting, getting a perfunctory nod from the sergeant at the counter just as the ever-smiling Marie Laval clicked over to us in her fashionable dress. "Mr. Wolfe, Mr. Goodwin, welcome once more. Please come back with me to the *commissaire*'s office."

Bouchard rose from behind his desk as we walked in. "Gentlemen, welcome. Monsieur Gervais is already seated, along with his lawyer, named Picard. Neither of them is happy to be here. As with our previous conversation, Lieutenant Allard will be taking notes."

For the second time during this narrative, I am sorry to have to present a portion of the story filtered through the voice of a translator, but it's my penance for not taking French in high school back in Ohio, as had been suggested by Mrs. Crockett, my counselor. I took Latin instead, don't ask me why.

I settled into the observation room with a cup of coffee supplied by Miss Laval and watched through the one-way glass as Bouchard, Allard, and Wolfe walked into interview room. The three were still standing when Gervais jumped up and pointed at Wolfe. "What is that man doing here?" he shouted while his lawyer tugged on his sleeve, trying to pull him down.

"Monsieur Wolfe is present at my invitation," he said calmly. "He is an adviser."

"What are his credentials?" Picard asked. "We were not told he would be present."

"What are your own credentials?" Bouchard fired back. "Are you licensed to practice law in France?"

That shut up the mouthpiece and the five settled in on the opposite long sides of the rectangular table: Allard, Bouchard, and Wolfe on one side, Gervais and his lawyer on the other. Bouchard motioned to his lieutenant to begin.

Allard: Present are Commissaire René Bouchard; Private Investigator Nero Wolfe; Monsieur Claude Gervais; Monsieur Jean Picard; and Lieutenant Pierre Allard. (Allard then gave the time and date and said the interview was being recorded.)

Gervais: Who is this Nero Wolfe? That is the man who came into my shop in Geneva on two occasions and tried to get me to press charges against a burglar. From the way he talked, I could tell he is neither Swiss nor French, although he speaks well. He claimed to be with some international organization.

Picard: Did he threaten you, Claude?

Gervais: Not in so many words, but he seemed to be dangerous. Also, he had a man with him who kept coming back to the store and staring in the window. It was very disconcerting.

Bouchard: Did that man threaten you at any time, or reenter your shop?

Gervais: No, but I was afraid of him.

Bouchard: Would you like to file charges against either of these gentlemen with the Swiss authorities?

Gervais: No, no, that is not necessary.

Bouchard: Then let us then move on to the reason for this meeting, Alto Chronometers, of which you are the president. Is that correct?

Gervais: (turning to his lawyer, who nodded) Yes, yes it is.

Bouchard: We would like you to explain why at least one of your Alto watches contains a movement that was smuggled into France.

Picard: Can you prove that allegation?

Bouchard: If all of this ever comes to trial, an expert witness will testify that an Alto product we examined had a movement made by MicroMetrics of Geneva and that it contained a serial number that was part of a series of these movements we confiscated from a man crossing into France from Switzerland. May I assume you have heard of MicroMetrics, Monsieur Gervais?

Gervais: Certainly. Alto uses their products. And I can't explain why the company's movements have been brought here in an apparently illegal way.

Wolfe: (to Bouchard) May I intercede?

Bouchard: You may, sir.

Wolfe: Mr. Gervais, when I was in your establishment in Geneva, I recall you telling me that you are the exclusive seller of another line of watches, Deltona. Is that true?

Gervais: (shifting nervously in his chair) Yes.

Wolfe: And during that conversation, you also stated the movements for the Deltona timepieces came from MicroMetrics. Is my memory correct?

Gervais: (looking at Picard, who shrugged) Uh . . . yes.

Wolfe: You seem to have a great deal of faith in the products of MicroMetrics. Do you have a direct connection with that manufacturer, sir?

Gervais: I . . . am . . . the owner of the company.

Wolfe: And what is your position at Deltona?

Gervais: (to Pichard) Am I obliged to answer?

Picard: No, this is not a courtroom.

Wolfe: Mr. Bouchard, I suggest that if you have someone delve into the Swiss records, you will find that Mr. Gervais is the owner, very likely the *sole* owner, of the Deltona organization.

Bouchard: If that is the case, what we have here is one individual operating rival watch companies as well as heading a firm that makes their innards, innards identified by an expert as being of an inferior quality.

Picard: On behalf on my client, I would like to know the identity of the individual who claims the MicroMetrics movements are of an inferior quality.

Bouchard: That can be arranged, although you should be aware that his credentials are of a sterling nature, so you risk ridicule. Mr. Wolfe, I believe you wish to continue.

Wolfe: I do, sir. There is much more to Mr. Gervais's story. First, some admitted speculation on my part: I believe his jewelry store in Geneva is not financially viable and bankruptcy may loom, although that is for others to determine. (At this point, Gervais stands up and shouts at Wolfe and Bouchard demands that he sit down. He does.)

Wolfe: To go on, Mr. Gervais has developed a plan to hold on to his store by starting a new company, Alto, which has just begun producing watches in the French town of Samoëns that contain movements produced by a new Swiss company, MicroMetrics, also owned by Mr. Gervais.

Bouchard: Wait a moment: What about those Deltona watches that Gervais already sells in his store?

Wolfe: What indeed? I believe you will find Deltona to be what in the United States is referred to as a "shell company" that was never intended to produce large numbers of watches. He was likely to have soon closed the operation.

Bouchard: Please explain the term "shell company."

Wolfe: This is an organization with no significant assets formed to secure financing for another company. I believe Deltona was created by Mr. Gervais so the MicroMetrics movements made for its watches could be used in Alto watches. Mr. Gervais, who never planned to sell many Deltona watches, made sure through his small number of employees that Deltona would automatically reject movements so that they then could be made available to Alto.

Bouchard: These then were the movements smuggled into France?

Wolfe: Precisely.

Bouchard: Mr. Gervais, how do you respond to this?

Picard: My client does not choose to comment.

Bouchard: France does not look kindly upon the establishment of businesses built by questionable means, or I should say in this case, *illegal* means. Our courts will have more to say about this. In the meantime, Mr. Pichard, we will be holding your client on a charge of smuggling. Mr. Wolfe?

Wolfe: You may want to add that charge, Commissionaire. Mr. Gervais's transgressions include kidnapping and murder.

Picard: I protest this outrageous performance on the part of a man who is neither a French nor a Swiss citizen nor a law enforcement officer.

Bouchard: We will take your protest under advisement, sir, despite the fact you cannot practice law in this country. Monsieur Wolfe, please continue.

Wolfe: I believe you will find Mr. Gervais has had at his disposal a number of men who carry out his orders and you probably will have to work with the Swiss police to unearth at least the solution of the unsolved shooting death of Lucien Leclerc in Geneva. Mr. Leclerc, a crew member on lake steamers, became suspicious of men riding between Geneva and Évian and may have been seen as a threat to Mr. Gervais's watchmaking enterprise in Samoëns.

Charles Moreau, who I believe you are still holding, had been arrested by Geneva police attempting to burglarize Mr. Gervais's store, but no charges were pressed against him, perhaps because his so-called burglary was an attempt by Mr. Gervais to collect insurance money for the jewelry while still having control of it.

Bouchard: I sense you are not done yet.

Wolfe: I am not. (Here, Wolfe's voice takes on a

hard-edged tone I had never before heard.) Men under Mr. Gervais's supervision kidnapped two men, Fritz Brenner and Paul Bernard, and almost surely would have killed them had they not escaped their captors.

Gervais: (Leaping to his feet and waving his hands) That is not true! They would have been freed as soon as—

Wolfe: As soon as your watchmaking operation in Samoëns was up and running?

That was it for Gervais. He had been increasingly jumpy as Wolfe continued to bore in on his actions and he now was slumped in his chair as Picard put an arm around him and whispered to him. Bouchard stood up as Lieutenant Allard said, "Interview concluded at . . ." giving the time and date.

CHAPTER 23

I was surprised that Gervais caved in so quickly, although he surely had seen the end coming for him. Bouchard and his opposite numbers with the Swiss police worked together and Gervais ended up getting tried—and convicted—in both countries.

The trials had not yet begun when Wolfe, Fritz, and I prepared to return to the United States, but we would later to learn that through a cooperative agreement, Claude Gervais ended up serving a life sentence in a Swiss prison for overseeing the murder of Lucien Leclerc, that charge being the most serious of several of which he had been found guilty. The man who did the actual shooting of Leclerc, named Pierre Didier, also got a life sentence. It was fortunate that both men were tried in Switzerland where there is no death penalty. Had the trials been in France, they each likely would have faced the guillotine.

Lesser sentences were doled out to Moreau and the men who were involving in the kidnapping of Fritz and Paul Bernard, although if it had been up to Wolfe, they, too, would be serving life sentences.

We had one last meeting with René Bouchard, this one in a small meeting room in our hotel. He had wanted to thank Wolfe for his help and he felt that, this time, he should be the one to travel between countries as a way to honor us.

"You must have suspected Gervais from the very start," Bouchard asked Wolfe as we all drank coffee.

"When Archie and I met him in his store, he seemed exceedingly obsequious and . . ."

Seeing Bouchard's confusion, Wolfe said, "I feel the need to better explain my usage. 'Obsequious' means fawning or unduly humble, as if putting on an act to ingratiate oneself."

"I understand," Bouchard said, nodding. "Hardly what one would term an endearing quality."

"Not at all. That trait made me immediately suspicious of him and from then on, I began to question everything we were to learn about him."

"I am still puzzled about how your Monsieur Brenner and his friend were able to escape from that house up in the hills above Évian."

"I gather from what they told us that they were finally able to overpower the people who held them," Wolfe replied in an even tone.

"Rather remarkable," Bouchard said, furrowing his brow. "They must have grappled over a pistol, with one of the two prisoners seizing it and shooting the captor in the struggle. This would seem to be a justifiable act, do you not think so?"

"I certainly do," Wolfe agreed. "Most justifiable."

CHAPTER 24

As I write this at my desk in the office, I can hear Wolfe and Fritz in the kitchen, arguing over something to do with anchovies. As is my usual practice, I will keep my distance during that contretemps, as an entry onto the battlefield would force me to take sides, a definite no-win situation. On the plus side, never did I imagine that their voices raised to each other would be such a welcome sound.

Fritz is slowly coming to look like his old self, gaining back the weight he had lost during his Swiss ordeal. He also has gotten over his funk about how disordered and dirty he found the kitchen in the wake of Leon Farber's tenure in the kitchen. Farber has gone back to his job at Rusterman's, as happy to be away from the brownstone as we are to see the last of him.

Lily seems to be delighted with the Swiss music box I brought back for her. It did not hurt my cause in the least that the piece of music in that box, Debussy's "Clair de Lune," is one of her favorites. And before you ask, I did not buy it at Claude Gervais's now-shuttered jewelry store.

In our absence, Saul managed the brownstone's operations with his usual efficiency and he was even able to solve a case of his involving a Long Island City department store clerk who was walking out after work every few days wearing a dress under her clothing.

Theodore, who probably moped around the greenhouse every day that we were away, has gone back to being the brownstone's resident fussbudget, constantly fretting about some real or imagined orchid disease and calling me from the plant rooms to ask if I think Wolfe is getting enough to eat.

"Why don't you direct that question to Fritz?" I snap. "I am not Mr. Wolfe's keeper."

Wolfe himself quickly returned to his pre-Switzerland routine as if he had never been away from home. One of his first acts upon our return was to huddle with Fritz and assess the state of the kitchen. They took stock of the situation and shook their heads over Leon Farber's disregard for the orderliness with which Fritz has always taken well-deserved pride.

Coming to Farber's defense, Saul told us the meals he was served were of decent quality, although he said that they certainly fell short of being up to Fritz's standards.

As we reacclimated to the regularity of life in the brownstone, Wolfe gradually began to view our jaunt to Switzerland as an adventure. Although when he now talks about those days with increasing nostalgia, he conveniently omits mentioning his discomfort on the long transatlantic flights or on those all-too-frequent tension-filled rides in the back seats of automobiles going from Geneva to and from France, many of them being driving by someone other than me.

And he never, not once, has referred to a gunshot fired in a small and shabby house nestled in the foothills of Mont Blanc.

AUTHOR'S NOTE

As with my previous Wolfe novels, I want to thank the estate of Rex Stout for graciously allowing me to continue the adventures of Nero Wolfe, Archie Goodwin, and the other recurring characters so brilliantly conceived by Mr. Stout.

I also give thanks to my agent, Martha Kaplan, as well as to Otto Penzler and Charles Perry of Mysterious Press and to the team at Open Road Integrated Media, all of whom have supplied advice, support, and encouragement.

And I reserve my most ardent thanks for my wife, Janet, to whom this story is dedicated. Without her, I long ago would have been adrift.

ABOUT THE AUTHOR

Photo Credit: Colleen Berg

Robert Goldsborough is an American author best known for continuing Rex Stout's famous Nero Wolfe series. Born in Chicago, he attended Northwestern University and upon graduation went to work for the Associated Press, beginning a lifelong career in journalism that would include long periods at the *Chicago Tribune* and *Advertising Age*. While at the *Tribune*, Goldsborough began writing mysteries in the voice of Rex Stout, the creator of iconic sleuths Nero Wolfe and Archie Goodwin. Goldsborough's first novel starring Wolfe, *Murder in E Minor* (1986), was met with acclaim from both critics and devoted fans, winning a Nero Award from the Wolfe Pack.

THE NERO WOLFE MYSTERIES

FROM MYSTERIOUSPRESS.COM
AND OPEN ROAD MEDIA

MYSTERIOUSPRESS.COM

MYSTERIOUSPRESS.COM

Otto Penzler, owner of the Mysterious Bookshop in Manhattan, founded the Mysterious Press in 1975. Penzler quickly became known for his outstanding selection of mystery, crime, and suspense books, both from his imprint and in his store. The imprint was devoted to printing the best books in these genres, using fine paper and top dust-jacket artists, as well as offering many limited, signed editions.

Now the Mysterious Press has gone digital, publishing ebooks through **MysteriousPress.com**.

MysteriousPress.com offers readers essential noir and suspense fiction, hard-boiled crime novels, and the latest thrillers from both debut authors and mystery masters. Discover classics and new voices, all from one legendary source.

FIND OUT MORE AT
WWW.MYSTERIOUSPRESS.COM

FOLLOW US:

@emysteries and Facebook.com/MysteriousPressCom

MysteriousPress.com is one of a select group of publishing partners of Open Road Integrated Media, Inc.

THE MYSTERIOUS BOOKSHOP, founded in 1979, is located in Manhattan's Tribeca neighborhood. It is the oldest and largest mystery-specialty bookstore in America.

The shop stocks the finest selection of new mystery hardcovers, paperbacks, and periodicals. It also features a superb collection of signed modern first editions, rare and collectable works, and Sherlock Holmes titles. The bookshop issues a free monthly newsletter highlighting its book clubs, new releases, events, and recently acquired books.

58 Warren Street
info@mysteriousbookshop.com
(212) 587-1011
Monday through Saturday
11:00 a.m. to 7:00 p.m.

FIND OUT MORE AT:

www.mysteriousbookshop.com

FOLLOW US:

@TheMysterious and Facebook.com/MysteriousBookshop

EARLY BIRD BOOKS

FRESH DEALS, DELIVERED DAILY

Love to read?
Love great sales?

Get fantastic deals on bestselling ebooks delivered to your inbox every day!

Sign up today at
earlybirdbooks.com/book